# THE LAND OF REM

(Reboot)

by

James S. Earl

**Gotham Books**

30 N Gould St.
Ste. 20820, Sheridan, WY 82801
https://gothambooksinc.com/

Phone: 1 (307) 464-7800

© 2024 *James S. Earl*. All rights reserved.

No part of this book may be reproduced, stored in a retrieval system, or transmitted by any means without the written permission of the author.

Published by Gotham Books (October 2, 2024)

ISBN: 979-8-3303-3834-4 (H)
ISBN: 979-8-3303-3830-6 (P)
ISBN: 979-8-3303-3831-3 (E)

Because of the dynamic nature of the Internet, any web addresses or links contained in this book may have changed since publication and may no longer be valid.

The views expressed in this work are solely those of the author and do not necessarily reflect the views of the publisher, and the publisher hereby disclaims any responsibility for them.

# Book Review for author...

In-house Book Reviewer

Writers' Branding LLC

Rating: ★★★★★

**Title: "The Land of REM": A Spellbinding Dream Odyssey that Speaks to the Soul**

"The Land of REM" is not merely a book; it's a journey into the recesses of the human spirit, a tapestry woven with the threads of dreams and the enigmatic realms of the subconscious. In the heart of this captivating narrative is Tim Stubbs, a guide through a dream world that blurs the lines between imagination and reality.

Tim's recurring dream—a stormy island with a mysterious mansion—serves as the portal to the Land of REM. Fueled by the courage born of a night of heavy drinking, he steps into this dream mansion—a place that transcends the ordinary and beckons him to explore the uncharted territories of his own mind. The revelation that Marvin, encountered within this dream realm, has slipped into a coma in the waking world creates a poignant bridge between reality and the fantastical Land of REM. This connection propels Tim into a daring decision— inducing his own coma to embark on a quest that transcends the boundaries of both dreams and wakefulness.

As the narrative unfolds, it weaves a seamless tapestry of mystery and fantasy, inviting readers to question the very fabric of their reality. Tim's journey becomes a metaphorical exploration of the human psyche, where dreams unfold as intricate dances between the conscious and the subconscious. Beyond the central odyssey, "The Land of REM" opens a treasure chest of short.

Inviting readers to question the very fabric of their reality. Tim's journey becomes a metaphorical exploration of the human psyche, where dreams unfold as intricate dances between the conscious and the subconscious.

Beyond the central odyssey, "The Land of REM" opens a treasure chest of short stories—each a gem that adds a layer of delight to the overarching narrative. From humor to the supernatural, science fiction, and a whimsical take on the Tooth Fairy, these stories offer a kaleidoscopic view into the multifaceted nature of human imagination.

This book isn't just about dreams; it's an ode to the human spirit's ceaseless yearning for understanding and connection. Tim Stubbs becomes not just a character but a vessel through which readers embark on a shared exploration of the mysterious landscapes within.

"The Land of REM" isn't a book; it's an immersive experience that reaches into the depths of the soul. With its masterful blend of mystery, fantasy, and short stories, it extends an invitation to every reader to delve into the profound mysteries of their own dreams.

Kobe Williams

Senior Book Reviewer

**WRITERS' BRANDING**

# The Land of REM

James S. Earl
Book Review from ForewordReviews
https://www.forewordreviews.com/reviews/the-land-of-rem/
Clarion Rating: 4 out of 5

Evocative details and strong science fiction themes make this short story collection fresh and intriguing.

In *The Land of REM* by James S. Earl, fantastical worlds are populated by vivid characters who beg to be revisited, all laid out with humor, compassion, and measured detail, with themes of time travel and transcendence running throughout.

*The Land of REM*, the titular novella in this collection of short stories, centers on the first stop that everyone takes on their journey through the afterlife. In REM some stay a while, some move on quickly, but most enter through the conventional lighted tunnel. There exists a pre-death back door, however, and Tim Stubbs manages to find it in a recurring dream. He meets a man there named Marvin, and after he wakes up, the man starts to impact his conscious life as well. Tim's only hope for figuring out what it all means is to find a way to return to the Land of REM. The implications of fantastical travel are a theme that runs through most of the other stories in the book as well.

Throughout the stories are memorable characters who stand out for their compassion and warmth. One is Professor Emit N. Relevart, who evokes the ghosts of Charles Dickens's *A Christmas Carol*, if with a much warmer and sympathetic personality, as he sends people through time and space in an effort to help them learn a lesson. The professor shows up in a few stories, sometimes as a protagonist, sometimes in a cameo.

Stories are composed with subtle beauty and sparse, perfectly chosen details. In "Felicia Nightingale," a squad in Vietnam is transported to one soldier's home in the Louisiana bayou after things go wrong on patrol. The man's dead wife is there and serves them home-brewed honey beer and a giant crawfish boil. Much of the story flows along on dialogue, but the small, simple details paint a complete picture of the setting, from the breeze through an open window to a hand on the shoulder.

Because there is such a strong theme of science fiction and fantasy in the titular story and elsewhere, the few stories that don't fit that genre feel out of place in the collection. This is most true of its single nonfiction piece, "The Tooth Fairy, God, and Everything Else" and the medical satire, "An Inconvenient Truth." While both stories are entertaining and engaging, their positions in the middle of the book feel like speed bumps in an otherwise smooth road.

*The Land of REM* will appeal to fans of science fiction and fantasy who enjoy thoughtful pieces with sly dialogue and memorable characters.

**Reviewed by Christine Canfield**

**April 7, 2016**

# KIRKUS REVIEW

**The Land of REM**
**by James S. Earl**
**RELEASE DATE: Oct. 3, 2013**

*A set of bedtime stories for adults that, much like their childhood counterparts, should leave the reader asking for more.*

Earl brings dreams, history, and beliefs together across time and space in this debut short story collection, a selection of literary fantasy tales.

To some extent, the stories in this volume all concern the worlds beyond the characters own, particularly the afterlife. The title work follows Tim Stubbs, a successful, happily married insurance executive. After a promotion and a lavish party, the last thing on the up-and-comer's mind should be a recurring dream. But when a claim comes across his desk for a man in a coma—Marvin Dispatcher, the same man he's seen in that dream—Tim can't ignore it. He quickly becomes obsessed, drawing connections between his life and Marvin's, eventually forcing himself into unconsciousness with scotch and Valium to return to the dream and the Land of REM. He encounters wonders and heroes there, as well as a mission that will change his life forever. Other stories in the collection, such as "Recall" and "Death Takes a Holiday," also meditate on death and the afterlife, while some, like the nonfiction piece "The Tooth Fairy, God, and Everything Else," address questions of faith, belief, and devotion. "The Land of REM" could certainly be expanded into a novel in its own right, but the contrast provided by the other stories also serves to heighten this central narrative. The tales simultaneously feel ethereal, comic, and personal. There are problems with awkward sentences and typographical foibles here and there (for example, "This was like a finally test of manhood"). These sorts of issues don't make much of an impact in the dreamlike sections, which deftly capture the stream-of-consciousness feeling of actual dreams and create a strong sense of place and tone. But the problems stand out in the more mundane content. There are many complex ideas at play throughout this collection. More time and words spent on this thin volume would go a long way toward exploring these notions fully and eliminating the troublesome elements.

A set of bedtime stories for adults that, much like their childhood counterparts, should leave the reader asking for more.

## The Land of REM

**James S. Earl**
**Book Review from Blue Ink Review**
https://www.blueinkreview.com/book-reviews/the-land-of-rem/

This interesting collection includes the title novella, along with 10 pieces of flash fiction, all of which explore the subjects of dreams, time travel, death, and spirituality. Recurrent themes (time is relative), images (life/death represented in dreamscapes), and the time-traveling character Professor Emit N. Relevart (who also appears as "Relevant") drift in and out of these stories.

The novella concerns Tim Stubbs, an uncaring insurance executive who meets one of his dying customers in a dream. When he learns this customer is comatose from brain cancer, Tim returns to the dream for more information. An experienced lucid dreamer, he manipulates the dream to meet important dead people from the past in The Land of REM.

The stories that follow include "Recall," in which a man attempts to bring his comatose wife back to life; "Death Takes a Holiday," where a prison guard describes his death experience; and "Felicia Nightingale," which focuses on a squad leader in Vietnam who regularly visits his dead wife. "Angel," an award-winning story according to a notation, tells of an inspirational encounter between two truckers meeting accidentally on a busy Texas highway. In addition, two stories written as personal essays offer a humorous look at colonoscopies and childhood mythology.

While the recurrent themes are intriguing enough to warrant exploration, without further depth or breadth in subsequent stories, recurrence becomes mere repetition. For instance, in the novella, Tim Stubbs awakens from a dream in which he eats an apple and finds "As he brushed his teeth a piece of apple skin came out in his spit" and later, in "Felicia Nightingale" a corporal endures a near-death experience during which he dreams of eating crawfish and awakens with a piece of crawfish shell stuck in his teeth. Numerous grammatical and spelling errors also distract from the storytelling.

Even so, this collection is entertaining overall and may appeal to short story and science fiction fans with interest in the aforementioned themes.

Also available in hardcover and eBook.

In Loving Memory of my Grandson

Samuel Thomas Scott

30 September 1992 – 6 October 2010

## *Table of Contents*

Epilogue...................................................................................xiv
The Party..................................................................................1
The Dream...............................................................................4
Strange Day.............................................................................10
Marvin......................................................................................15
Hospital....................................................................................17
Meeting with the Boss..........................................................20
Bill.............................................................................................23
REM Revisited.......................................................................26
The Platform..........................................................................30
South Village..........................................................................33
Grandma.................................................................................36
Meeting with Marvin...........................................................40
The Map..................................................................................42
Doc Holliday..........................................................................44
The Map Revisited...............................................................48
Jesus.........................................................................................50
Return Home.........................................................................52
Hospital, Act II......................................................................55
Thanksgiving Dinner..........................................................57
Medical Report.....................................................................59
Blue Jay of Happiness.........................................................61
Epilogue (This time I mean it).........................................62
*Recall*........................................................................................69
*Death Takes a Holiday*........................................................76
*God, The Tooth Fairy, and Everything Else* ....................82
*Angel*........................................................................................88
*An Inconvenient Truth (What? It's Wrong When I Say It)*............95
*Fishing on Belton Lake with John Wesley Hardin*........100
*The Professor*........................................................................107
*The Professor Two*...............................................................115
*The Professor Three*............................................................131

| | |
|---|---|
| *Character* | 148 |
| *Whoops!* | 153 |
| *Flower Effect* | 156 |
| *Homecoming* | 161 |
| *Rally* | 168 |
| *Felicia Nightingale* | 175 |

# Epilogue

For the time travelers among you, just a word to let you know that John Stubbs is doing well. He graduated Harvard Medical School with honors in 2028. He founded the Land of REM Foundation in 2056, and became its chairman upon his death in 2092. He sends his regards to all Land of REM members. You may not be familiar with the whole story, so I have titled the chapters for you to go right where you need to go. I cover some of the little known facts that I received from John's dad, the last time I was in the Land of REM. Naturally the account stops shortly after John's birth, because all that followed is pretty much common knowledge.

One edition of this printing, the first if you look at it chronologically, was published in the early part of the twenty-first century. Most of the readers were not time travelers. As I think back, I wasn't a time traveler. The Land of REM was basically undiscovered in the mortal realm. We were content, for the most part, to move through time in a forward only, linear progression. Our hindsight was twenty-twenty, and our foresight was blind as a bat. For those people I say, forget about John. He is a baby now, and has no bearing on the story. This is a tale about his dad, Tim Stubbs. Tim was able to travel in the Land of REM, and come back to tell about it. Since you probably don't even know what the Land of REM is, don't feel bad, I didn't either then, this book may be viewed as the introduction to the Land of REM. Therefore, for your edition I have titled it *The Land of REM*.

I strongly suggest that the later mentioned people, start at the beginning with Chapter One, and read sequentially through to the end. In fact, you shouldn't even read the epilogue. Why would you read the epilogue first? Oh well, happy reading. I hope you enjoy the story.

# The Party

Tim Stubbs put his book down on the end table, and called to his wife, "Honey, did you know that Doc Holliday had reoccurring dreams in which he actually met the people he had killed?"

Kate Stubbs entered the living room while still taking the rollers out of her hair. She was still in her slip. This let Tim know that he had at least thirty minutes before they would be ready to leave. She looked at him quizzically, and reached over to pick up the book.

"You actually found a book on Doc Holliday that you have not read before?" she asked while picking up the book. Her husband was a totally and thoroughly dedicated Doc Holiday fan.

"It's way off the beaten path, and not many copies were published," Tim said.

Kate looked at the book and read aloud, "*Doc Holiday and the Alternate Universe*. By Emit N. Relevant." She giggled. Tim chuckled back.

"I told you," he said.

"The desperation of an addict," she teased.

"Guilty as charged," Tim muttered.

She gave him a big smile, leaned over, and planted a noisy kiss on top of his head. She left passion pink lip prints on his bald spot. She giggled, and wiped them off with her wrist. Then, as an afterthought, she licked the remaining lip stick off the top of his head. Tim scrunched up his body and started to giggle.

"Don't start anything you can't finish," he said with mock sternness.

"Hey, you get your promotion present from me after the party," Kate said as she turned, and walked out of the room. At the door she said, "I'll be ready in fifteen minutes."

Tim smiled, and picked up his book. He now knew that he had over an hour before she would be ready. Enough time to finish his book.

One hour and twenty minutes later Kate returned to the living room looking stunning. Tim smiled and kissed her lightly on her cheek being careful not to mar the makeup.

"I'll drive," she said. "My Chief Executive should enjoy himself tonight."

And enjoy himself was what Tim did. His boss, James Vernon Cherry the third, or Jimbo, as his inner circle called him was big into the party scene. A self-made multi-millionaire, he had created Galaxy Life from a struggling lending agency. Just recently he had added a medical insurance branch with Tim selected to be its Chief Executive. Tim was not much of a drinker, but Jimbo not only forgave heavy partying, he insisted on it. At least for his inner circle people. So Tim, always dutiful, always the perfectionist, gave it his best shot.

Tim did not remember much about the party. It was held in his honor to celebrate his promotion within the ranks of Galaxy Life, with special thanks for taking on the medical insurance branch. They were all inner circle people there. This was like a final test of manhood. He had eight drinks before he made his acceptance speech, and about ten afterwards.

Kate poured him into the car, got him home, and upstairs to bed. She even managed to get him out of his clothes. The only clear memory of that evening for Tim was Kate snuggling into bed next to him.

"I guess I'll have to give you your present later," she said and kissed him passionately. Then sighed, and kissed him on his forehead.

Tim lost consciousness thinking what a lucky man he was to have Kate. He had completely forgotten about his promotion.

# The Dream

Tim was having that dream again. The one in which he was falling. No, flying would be more accurate, for he could control his descent. He was headed toward a small tropical island. A hurricane was brewing, with twenty foot waves crashing onto the shore. The sky was dark, and you could sense the wind, but it was all visual. Tim could not feel the wind or rain as he crashed toward the island. He did notice that the closer he got the slower he fell. He had this dream a few times before when he was a child. He remembered it even though it had been over twenty years since he had last dreamed it. His mind struggled to recall the reality of the situation.

Kate had poured him into bed last night. They had been at a party in Dallas. It was a big wig affair with his work at the *Galaxy Life Insurance Company*. He had just received a promotion and his boss had told him to loosen up and enjoy the evening. Tim took the advice to heart. His wife, always supportive, had kept him out of trouble, driven him home, and put him to bed. He had immediately passed out. Now he was dreaming.

But this time he was able to fly around the island and check it out. The island was approximately one mile in diameter. Its shores were lined with jagged rocks which now had huge waves crashing on them. There was no beach. Where the rocks ended, a velvet grass, similar to a golf course putting green, started. This covered the whole island except for periodically spaced palm trees, and of course, the house or more like a mansion.

A giant two story house sat in the dead center of the island. The first floor was modern, in a rich playboy mansion kind of way. It was all very normal, but the second floor terrified him. It was a dilapidated structure, with broken windows, that reminded him of every haunted house he had ever seen. Tim could see ghostly figures moving about through the broken windows, and knew from previous dreams that this was where the nightmares were kept.

With sheer will power he forced myself down to the first floor, and landed on the front door stoop.

"Beats walking," Tim said out loud. His voice had a tinny sound, like it was from a speaker of an old movie projector.

Above the door was a plaque that read, this is the *Portal to the Land of REM*. Summoning up his courage, Tim opened the door and stepped inside.

He entered the living room area of a small modern townhouse. Startled he leaped back and landed outside. Looking up he was staring at the Hugh Hefner Jack the Ripper Haunted Playboy Mansion again. He had never entered the house in any of the previous dreams. This was freaking him out. After several deep breathes he gathered his courage and stepped back through the door.

Back in the town house. It contained a couch, two chairs, a coffee table, an entertainment center complete with TV, and a desk containing a computer. The overhead light was already on and Tim walked across the carpeted floor to explore more of the house. Behind the living room, through an open doorway, was the kitchen. It was modern in all respects to include a micro wave oven. Tim opened the refrigerator and discovered it was stocked. He grabbed an apple and continued through the house.

Eating his apple, Tim headed left into a full, but small, bathroom. He had been drinking all night, so he stopped at the toilet and took a leak. A horrible thought crossed his mind. He realized he was dreaming and had probably just taken a leak in his bed. Kate will be very mad. Oh well, it would not be the first time, that she was mad at him. Tim was not a control freak, but he had not peed the bed since he was three. Oh well, nothing he could do about it now anyway, he thought, as he continued eating his apple, and headed up toward the front of the house through an open door.

Tim entered a bedroom that contained a water bed. Next to the water bed was a nightstand with a clock radio. The clock read 3:04 AM. Tim opened a door to his left and entered a hallway. Across the hall he could see the living room. Having already explored that already, he turned to his right, and headed down the hallway toward a large staircase.

The main part of the staircase led up, toward the nightmares. Hesitantly, Tim headed up the steps. As he ascended, the steps went from fresh new carpeting to decayed and rotten. His feet seemed to sink into them. He stopped before he got to the top. He had seen the nightmares before, but a new one appeared at the top of the steps. A large breasted naked women beckoned him up. She was attractive, except for the fact that she had been disemboweled and her entrails hung loosely down in front of her. There was also an ax stuck in the side of her head. Her erotic nature made the gore even more horrifying. As if this horror was not enough, a fat headed boy with a fish hook stuck in his eye appeared beside her. He had snot running out of both nostrils. Tim was not in the mood for nightmares, no matter how exotic they may be. He turned around and rapidly headed downstairs.

As Tim approached the landing, the front door burst open, and a small man in a hospital gown rushed in. He ran into the hallway and seeing Tim he stopped.

"Hi," he said. "My name is Marvin. I have never seen anybody here before."

"Hi," Tim replied. "I'm Tim. This is my first time here." He was amazed at what a strange twist his dream had taken. He was also happy to be away from the nightmares.

"Well, got to go," Marvin said. He maneuvered around Tim and headed to the side of the stairwell. There he opened a door and headed down a previously hidden stairway.

Tim approached the door and looked down. It wound down into the abyss. He stared down after him for a few moments, but he really was not in the mood for nightmares. That place looked like it could have nightmares. Tim closed the door and headed back to the bedroom.

The clock radio read 4:07 AM. He finished his apple, which was already starting to turn brown, and threw it in the trash can. It was amazing the details his dream was producing. Tim headed to the living room. The desk top computer was flashing a prompt.

"Hi," Tim typed.

"Hi yourself," came the response.

"Who are you?" Tim asked.

"I am you," came back the typed response.

"You are Tim Stubbs?" Tim typed.

"In one respect, yes," came the reply.

"Is this my dream?" Tim typed back.

"Yes, along with others," came the response.

"Who was that strange man that just came in?" Tim queried.

"That was Marvin," came the reply.

"I know that!" Tim shouted out loud. "But who is Marvin?"

The computer prompt sat there flashing. Tim typed the question onto the screen.

"Marvin is that man who just came in," was the reply.

"Screw you!" Tim shouted and cut off the power switch. The computer remained on, but Tim ignored it. He walked back into the bedroom. The clock radio read 5:59 AM. If that clock was right, he had to get up in a minute anyway. Tim laid down on the bed and closed his eyes. Just for a second.

A loud buzzing sound woke him up. He was in his own bedroom and the alarm was blaring. It was 6:00 AM.

# Strange Day

Tim slammed off the alarm and quickly checked himself to see if he had wet the bed. Much to his surprise he hadn't. Tim was puzzled, his bladder felt empty. That was a first for a morning following a night of heavy drinking. He felt all around, dry. Kate started stirring and reached over and stroked Tim's belly.

"What luck," he thought. "I guess she wasn't mad at me after all."

"Congratulations on your promotion," Kate said, as her hand moved lower.

"Thank you," Tim said. For a brief moment his thoughts drifted to an attractive, large breasted, disemboweled woman with an ax stuck in her head.

Fortunately, he was able to repress these thoughts and they made love in a slow and easy manner. It was tender and satisfying at the same time. When they were done Tim realized his luck was still holding, the clock read 6:30. He had missed his work out period at the gym and had to go straight to the showers. As he brushed his teeth a piece of apple skin came out in his spit.

"Honey," Tim said. "Did I eat any apples last night?"

"No," she replied. "You went straight for the booze."

"You sure? You could have missed it you know," he asked.

"No," came her reply. "I keep tight tabs on you. You are my man."

Tim was running late now so he didn't pursue it. He quickly dressed and headed off to work at Galaxy Life. Traffic was busy on Interstate Highway 635, as normal for that time of day, but he rode the shoulder, was very aggressive, and made it to work only ten minutes late.

"Good morning sir," Beth, Tim's new secretary said as he got off the elevator. "Welcome to your new office."

"Thank you, dear," Tim said, accepting a cup of coffee, and entered his office. There was a large stack of manila envelopes on the center of his desk. Tim noticed with satisfaction that his framed photograph of Doc Holiday had made it to his new office. He sat down at his brand new swivel chair and gave the photo an affectionate pat. Tim then rotated his chair to the back of the office where a large window gave him a magnificent twelve story view. A blue jay sat on the ledge. The bird looked up at Tim for a moment, and then winked. Startled, Tim quickly swiveled back to his desk. The stack of folders awaited him.

He grabbed one folder out of the middle and threw it to the side. That one would be last. He grabbed another one and opened it up. This one would be first. Some old lady needed approval for hand surgery because of her carpal tunnel operation. Tim denied it.

You don't need use of your hands at ninety-two. He had the stock holders to think of.

He worked through lunch. By 3:00 PM he was down to his last file. Beth entered carrying a stack of new files.

"Just set them over there," Tim said. She grunted and dropped them in the in box. Tim opened up the last file. Some old man needed a new liver. Tim denied it. Forty percent capacity was all a ninety-seven-year-old man needed for his liver. The company would reconsider when his liver functioning ability reached ten percent. Tim did work for the stock holders. Stamping the folder with the red "denied" stamp, He threw it in the pile. His first day at his promotion and he had already saved the company close to a million dollars. He might not come cheap, but he was worth every penny. Tim was way ahead of the game. That's why he got the big bucks. He just wished he didn't feel so bad about doing the right thing. His stomach was always hurting him lately.

Tim grabbed the new stack and picked one at random and threw it to the side. It would be last. He then grabbed another one out of the middle and opened it.

Tim's heart skipped a beat. There staring up at him, was a one by one inch, picture of Marvin.

"Could the man in my dreams be real?" Tim wondered. He read the folder. Marvin was a brain cancer patient who had gone into a coma at approximately 4:00 AM this morning. The company wanted Tim to investigate because life support would cost a fortune and the doctors did not think the man would recover. An attached sticky note explained that Galaxy Life would not recommend extensive life support.

But it was Marvin, the man in his dreams. To make matters more intense, he went into a coma about the same time Tim saw him in that strange house. What was that called? Tim racked his brains and then it came to him, the portal to the Land of REM.

"Beth," Tim called. "Cancel all my appointments today, I will be involved in this one case."

"Yes sir," came the reply. "What case is that?"

"Case 3141," Tim replied. "Marvin Dispatcher," he said, as he read the name off the folder.

Tim got up and closed the door. He moved all the other folders back into their pile in the in-box. Tim spent the rest of the afternoon studying about Marvin.

Marvin Dispatcher was a sixty-two-year-old white male, currently in a coma. He was being kept alive by life support equipment in a hospital in Temple, Texas. He had been diagnosed with brain cancer about two years ago. Six months ago he went into the hospital for a second surgery. He had lapsed into a comma that had lasted for a week. He had made some recovery but had gone comatose again this morning. This time, the doctors thought, for good. They saw no benefit to extended life support. Marvin had a sixty-year-old wife, Georgia, a thirty-two-year-old son, Bill, a daughter-in-law, Sarah, and a six-year-old granddaughter, Reba.

Tim sat lost in thought. Temple, that was only about a hundred miles south of here. He made up his mind.

"Beth," Tim called.

"Yes sir," she said, instantly appearing.

"I am going to go personally check out this Marvin Dispatcher case, in Temple. I am leaving tonight and I might not be in tomorrow. Keep me covered here."

"Yes sir," she said giving a mock salute.

Now for the hard part, Tim picked up the phone and called Kate. She took it rather well. She was such a good wife. He grabbed the file, got in his car and headed south on Interstate 35. Tim had to see Marvin in person. It had now become an obsession for him.

# Marvin

As Tim drove, he reviewed in his mind the files he had read on Marvin. Tim had even checked out the secret file, a file that supposedly did not exist. That file had contained some important information that could allow the company to deny the claim. Tim had removed it. He had not only removed the file, but he had felt good about doing it. Tim felt confused. He had always been a by the book, company first, type of guy. Now he felt strangely protective of this Marvin fellow. A man he had never met. Well, except once in a dream.

Marvin Dispatcher had been a truck driver. Twenty years ago, in 1981, he had rolled his truck, giving himself a concussion, and knocking himself out for over twelve hours. Marvin now had a form of brain cancer, but had not mentioned this possible pre-existing condition on his insurance application. If Galaxy Life were to innocently discover this fact, then they could have grounds to cancel the policy. At worst, they could at least tie it up in court for several years. Tim patted the file next to him. Of course that wouldn't happen if the file were to disappear. Tim had some decisions to make.

Tim gave a startled swerve as he remembered, 1981 was the year he had had his head injury. Another strange coincidence. Tim had been a young boy, and fallen out of a tree. He too had had a concussion and been knocked out for several hours.

Tim racked his brain for other coincidences. Marvin was married. What was her name? That's right, Georgia Dispatcher. Tim was married.

Marvin had a kid, a boy, thirty-two-year-old Bill. Tim had no children, but was in his thirties. He had turned thirty-three last November.

They were debating a hospital bill, Marvin's kid was named Bill. Tim chuckled. He was really grasping for straws now. Tim reached over and turned on the radio. He had to clear his mind. It was best to not form to many opinions until after he had investigated the situation.

# Hospital

Tim arrived at the hospital about eight that night. He entered Marvin's room and was greeted by an old lady. A young teary eyed girl clutched her leg. Tim looked over at the bed, and there lay Marvin. The Marvin he had met the night before in the Land of REM.

"Mrs. Georgia Dispatcher?" Tim asked.

"Yes," she said timidly, a questioning look in her eye.

"I'm Tim Stubbs, from Galaxy Insurance. I just came by to see how your husband was doing. This must be Reba."

"May I help you Mr. Stubbs?" she asked, suspicion in her voice.

"I just came to see how he was doing," Tim used his best pacifying tone.

"He is dying," she said. "He might as well be dead now." Georgia Dispatcher broke into tears. Reba stuck her head around her Grandma's leg.

"You're mean," Reba said.

Tim dropped down to one knee and looked at the little girl. This was why smart insurance men did not go visit patients. You cannot make wise decisions if you become personally involved.

"I just wanted to see him," Tim said.

"You can't see him here," Reba said. "He's not here. He is in the Land of REM."

Tim's heart almost stopped. "What did you say?" he shouted as he grabbed her. His composure was almost completely gone.

Georgia grabbed Tim's shoulder and started to push him away from her granddaughter.

"Stop it!" She cried. "Just get out of here!"

"But she said the Land of REM."

"She is just a little girl Mr. Stubbs. Now please, leave us alone."

"But the Land of REM, do you know of it?" Tim asked.

"Do I have to call for the nurse?" she asked.

The situation had gotten way out of hand. With great effort Tim fought to control myself.

"No," Tim said. He stood up and forced himself calm. "I just wanted to see him. The doctors are recommending that we don't continue life support."

"I don't see a need," Mrs. Dispatcher said. "He has a brain tumor with no chance of recovery. Let him go in peace. Let us get on with our lives." She then burst into tears, covering her face with her hands and making soft mewing sounds.

"I'm sorry," Tim said. He took a good long look at Marvin, lying unconscious on the bed. There were tubes all over. They were in his nose, his mouth, stuck in both arms, and many running under the sheets to God knows where. But it was, without a doubt, the same Marvin he had seen in his dream. He had gone downstairs in that dreamland called REM. Downstairs, a place Tim had never been. There was also the granddaughter Reba's comment. Tim could not let this rest in peace. He had to know.

But his fight was not here, not now. Tim turned and left the room. He did a lot of thinking on the two-hour drive back home. Marvin would have to stay alive until he could get some answers

## Meeting with the Boss

"Come in Tim," Jimbo said as he ushered Tim into his office. "Congratulations on your promotion to the twelfth floor. I see you saved us close to a million dollars on your first day." He walked over to the living room section of his office and sat down in one of the two plush leather covered chairs.

"Thank you sir," Tim said and sat in the other chair.

"Tim," he said, paused, and then gave a long sigh. "I'm confused on this other case of yours."

"Marvin Dispatcher, the coma case in Temple, Texas," Tim said. He had had a feeling when he was summoned that this was what this meeting was about.

"Yes," he smiled. "Good ole Tim, cut right to the chase. I don't understand why we, Galaxy Life, would agree to pay for additional life support treatment, when the doctors, and hell, even the family doesn't want it. That seems like poor business to me."

"Sir," Tim said, assuming a formal posture. "I have a feeling the doctors are wrong."

Jimbo rubbed his hands on the side of his head for a few moments and then said, "Galaxy Life is a profit making business. We are not life savers." He held up his hand to prevent interruption. "Let us go out on a limb here and say that you, an insurance man, know more about this situation than the doctors do. It makes no difference. His expenses are greater than the premium he is paying. They will in most probability remain that way for as long as he might live. A good business decision would be to cut our loss now. I know you know this." He leaned back in his chair.

Tim's mind raced as he thought about what to say. He couldn't tell him the truth. Galaxy Life didn't have crazy people working on the twelfth floor. Stalling for time Tim said, "It is rather personal, sir."

"You little dog," Jimbo said. A gleam came to his eye as he leaned forward again. "You're screwing someone in the family aren't you?" He gave a short laugh.

The preverbal light bulb went off in Tim's head. This was his way out. This was how he was going to learn about Marvin and the Land of REM. "Yes sir," Tim said. "Please, don't let Kate know."

"Tim," Jimbo said, nodding at him and giving a knowing smile. "If you continue to make us lots of money, we can allow certain perks in the job. However, this is an expensive perk. You need to get her out of your system. You have four days, till Monday. Then we must pull the plug on your tail bait."

"Yes sir," said Tim. He got up, gave a mock salute, and departed the office. Next stop Temple, but first he had to pick up some supplies.

# Bill

There where no objections from Jimbo, for Tim to take the rest of the day off to head down to Temple. God, fate, or whatever had given him the perfect cover story. He had to get in touch with the granddaughter. The home address would be the best place to start.

Tim arrived at their house about 3:00 P.M. No one was home. As he waited, he contemplated his actions. Jimbo had said three days before he pulled the plug. But he had also said Monday. It was now Thursday afternoon. He probably meant that Tim would have all day Friday plus the weekend to figure this out. Nothing would be changed till Monday morning.

"What do I do after I visit the granddaughter?" Tim wondered. "Another trip to REM?" Tim had to take it a step at a time. He was good at solving things. That's why they paid him the big bucks.

At 5:15 a car pulled into the drive. A lone man, a younger version of Marvin, got out. Might as well start here Tim thought.

"Mr. Bill Dispatcher," Tim said, extending his hand.

"Whoa," he said, startled. "And who are you?"

"Tim Stubbs, Galaxy Life," Tim said and grabbed his hand, shaking it. "I wanted to talk to you about your father."

"It's okay," he said. "We've agreed to sign the papers. We are not going to fight this."

"But you might want to," Tim said. "I had a dream about your father and the Land of REM."

Bill stared at Tim for a moment with a surprised look on his face. "Would you like to come in, Mr....?"

"Stubbs. But call me Tim."

"Okay, Tim," Bill said and guided him toward the house.

Tim followed him into the living room. The whole time Bill kept glancing at him. They sat down on the couch.

"Why did you say Land of REM?" Bill asked.

"I had a dream that I was in the Land of REM," Tim started. He figured honesty would be the best course of action. "I met your father there. He arrived at about the same time he went into a coma. Then the next day I see his file at work. Also, your daughter..."

"Yes, Reba," he said. "I heard about what happened."

"Right, Reba," Tim continued. "She said he was in the Land of REM. This has got me kind of crazy. I thought you, or her, might shed some light on this."

He was silent for a good minute. Finally he said, "When Dad came out of his first coma, he talked about this place. He called it the Land of REM. He said you entered through a portal that was actually a house. You had to go through a tunnel, and then you were in this village where all these dead people lived. It was the ramblings of a man with brain cancer who had just come out of a coma. But my daughter, who is six, was taken with the story. We didn't pay much attention to it. But I must say, your knowing of it has peaked my curiosity. Could such a place be real? Dad made it sound so real."

"I don't know," Tim said. "But I must find out. Can you give me some time?"

"Sure," Bill said. "If it doesn't hurt my family. What is it you want me to do?"

"Just don't let them pull the plug before Monday," I said. "Galaxy will foot the bills till then."

"But what do you plan to do?" Bill asked.

"I plan to go back," Tim said. "Back to the Land of REM."

Tim called Kate from Bill's house, and told her he would not be home until late Monday. That it was office stuff that couldn't wait. As always, she was understanding. Tim then bought himself a pint of Scotch and checked into a motel in downtown Temple. Before he entered the room, he grabbed the eight Valium from his AAA, special, "wink, wink" auto first aid kit.

Naked, with the TV blaring, Tim took the last valium with the last swig of Scotch. He had to take a leak, but what the hell; he could do that in the Land of REM. Darkness closed around him. He thought he might have cut the TV off. It didn't matter. He was having that dream again. The one in which he was falling, no flying would be more accurate.

## REM Revisited

The storm was still raging from his last visit. Tim immediately flew to the stoop on the first floor and landed feet first. He was becoming quite the expert at this. Above the door, still read the sign, *This is the Portal to the Land of REM*. He entered and headed to the computer.

"Where is Marvin?" Tim typed.

"The Land of REM," came the reply.

"How do I get there?" Tim asked.

"The fastest route for you would be to go downstairs," the screen answered.

"How far?" Tim typed.

"Through the ages," answered the computer.

Tim was starting to get annoyed with this computer and its cryptic answers. He figured the best way to find out anything was to just go exploring. Tim admitted to himself that he was a little nervous about what was below.

"Thanks for nothing. You have been a big help," Tim said aloud. He did not wait to see if there was a reply, but headed to the stairwell.

Tim opened the door at the base of the stairwell and looked down. It was dark down there and he was extremely nervous. This might be a dream, but, at this moment, he considered it more real than his waking life. He closed the door and went to the kitchen to try and find a flashlight. He found one in the kitchen and clicked it on. It worked and he headed back to the stairs to start his journey downward. It was a dark wooden stairway that turned and curved out of sight at the landing, about twenty steps downward. Tim's flashlight beam picked up some of all twenty steps in a dull beam, or he could concentrate it on about two or three steps in a brighter, more intense beam. Tim noticed that the steps appeared to get older as they descended. After several minutes of this visual exploring, Tim took a deep breath, and headed downward. Tim moved quickly, forcing himself downward in a deliberate fashion. As he turned the landing he could see the next floor.

The first thing Tim noticed about this new level was that the floor plan was the same as the one above, except it just seemed older. As he explored the new level he could see that it was as if he had stepped back in time. In the kitchen he set down the flashlight and turned on the kitchen lights. They were a gas operated lighting system. The kitchen had a wood burning stove and an old ice box. Tim opened the ice box, and no inside light came on. He could still make out that it was stocked with food. However, it was different food. It was fresh, but as if it came from a different time. It appeared as if the whole floor was somewhere out of the nineteenth century. The kitchen sink had a hand pump attached to it. Tim gave it a few pumps and cold water pumped into the sink. He went to grab the flashlight and stopped. His heart was pounding. The flashlight was gone. In its place was a lantern. His hands shaking, he found some matches in a drawer, and lit the lantern. He picked it up, and headed into the living room.

The living room was also lit with gas lighting. The desk was in the same place as before except that it was an older model. It wasn't an antique, it was in new condition; it was just built earlier. Instead of a computer, it had a quill pen and some writing paper on it. Tim went to the front door and tried to open it. It would not open. He went back to the desk and picked up the quill pen.

Tim stuck it in the ink well and wrote, "Why can't I open the door?"

Words started to appear on the paper just below where he had just penned the question.

"Not your time, you cannot leave through this level," they said.

"What time? What level?" Tim wrote back.

"You are in the portal to the Land of REM. You can only enter or exit through your own time. You may, however, pass through earlier portals, but not future portals," appeared the answer.

"Where is Marvin?" Tim wrote.

"He is already through the portal and in the Land of REM."

"How do I get there?" Tim asked.

"Downstairs, through the ages," came the reply.

Tim grabbed the lantern and headed down stairs. At the next level was a similar floor only even older. His lantern had turned into a torch. It was like he was in an old Colonial home. A fireplace lit the room. Tim wanted to explore this level, but he felt a sense of urgency. He had to keep moving. He must get to the Land of REM. He continued down to the next level.

Each level was older. Tim descended some sixty floors and arrived at a cave. There were paintings of animals on the wall. The kitchen consisted of a fire hearth with some large animal bones around it. There was no front door but the cave had an exit through the rear.

The stairs going down had finally ended. Building up his nerve, Tim walked through the back of the cave and entered a long tunnel. His torch had disappeared, but he could see a light at the end of the tunnel. Tim started walking toward the light. As he approached the light a man appeared at the entrance. He was smiling broadly, and that smile is what first let Tim recognize him. It made his head spin. Of all the weird things he had witnessed, this was the most bazaar, and yet the most wonderful. Tim started running toward the man. Tim had not cried sense he was thirteen years old, but he could not help himself. Tears streamed down his face as he rushed toward the man and gave him a big embrace. They stood hugging each other as Tim sobbed into the man's big broad shoulders. The last time Tim had seen this man was at his funeral, when Tim was only thirteen years old. He was Tim's Grandfather.

# The Platform

"Hi, Tim," Granddad said and gave him a big hug. "Not many people enter from this way."

Tim held on to him with a big hug, and continued to weep. His grandfather had been the most important person in his life. His grandfather allowed him his moment, and did not speak for a while. Finally, he separated himself from Tim, held him at arm's length, and looked him over with that appraising gaze Tim always loved as a child.

"Tim," he said. "You are looking very fit. It is so great to see you." He gently took his arm and guided him to a bench. "I'm glad you are here."

"But where is here?" Tim asked. He looked around. It appeared as if he was in a giant train or subway station. They were sitting on one of many benches that lined the walls of a very large platform. People were floating down a tunnel. A tunnel similar to one you would expect to see in a subway station. Except there were no tracks, and it radiated a bright light. People were floating down the tunnel on the bright beam of light. They would float down the center of the tunnel, and up to the platform where other people met them, and escorted them away. Some took time to sit on the benches like Granddad and Tim were doing. Some were hugging, or kissing, or laughing, or weeping. It was all a very emotional scene. There were hundreds of people in the station. Some people were entering the station, some exiting, but the flow of tunnel floaters remained. Sometimes the flow was heavier than other times, but always people floated through the tunnel.

"This is the platform," Tim's grandfather said. "This is where the newly deceased link up with their guide to the *Land of REM*. Usually their guide is someone they knew and trusted, a loved one. From here they go into the South Village. Some stay there for just a short while. Others live in the South Village for centuries."

"Am I dead?" Tim ask.

"No,' Granddad said with a chuckle. "You are dreaming. That's why you came in through one of the portals. It happens occasionally. I'm very proud of you. One out of a billion people find their way to the *Land of REM* without having to die first. The fact that one such person is my grandson has given me some powerful bragging rights." He gave Tim another broad smile and hugged Tim to him. "Let's go see Grandma."

They walked with a group of people up a stairway. Most everybody was firmly grounded by the time they left the platform. They exited into a beautiful meadow and crossed a bridge over a large babbling brook. Benches lined the pathway. Many of them had couples sitting and talking on them. Time seemed to be relaxed. Nobody was rushed, or in a hurry. Finally, Tim was able to pin point it, there was no stress. It was as if there was all the time in the world.

They continued down the path, and it curved between two hills. As they made their way down the path, the valley below came into view. Tim caught his breath.

There before him was a tremendous village. It stretched for miles and miles. No building, that he could see, was over two stories high, but there were literally millions of buildings. What really impressed him was how clean everything was. The sun was shining, like on the best of a spring day, and everything was glistening clean. Shops and houses lined the paths. They were from all manner of times and places. A fifth century hovel stood next to a twentieth century brick house. There was a candle shop from early America, and down the street was an old Roman pub. Tim walked in amazed silence. Granddad led the way.

# South Village

As they walked, Tim noticed that Granddad seemed a few years younger. He appeared like Tim remembered him looking when Tim was nine, and they had taken a trip to San Antonio. That had been a great day for Tim. It was just him and Granddad. On an adventure, as Granddad would say. They had toured the Alamo, and walked the entire River Walk. They had even visited a magic shop, and Tim had learned a trick with a ball and cup.

Granddad stopped, slowly turned, and gave Tim a big smile.

"Would you like to go on an adventure?" Granddad asked.

"Yes, Granddad," Tim said in a nine-year-old voice.

Granddad held out his hand and clasped Tim's hand. They walked a few paces in silence.

"Grandma can wait an hour, she won't mind," Granddad said. "Besides, this is a spiritual place. Time is felt differently here. We will get home at just the right time, no matter what time that is."

They walked hand in hand, just as they had in San Antonio decades ago, Granddad about half a pace in the lead, and explaining the sites. That was because Granddaddy had been there before. He knew the way, and he was willing to share with his grandson. Tim felt loved and secure. They turned a corner onto a cobblestone street.

"This is one of my favorite spots. It's the old Roman section," Granddad said.

Tim looked around wide eyed. "Where are the coliseums and statues?"

"Remember, this is a spiritual place," Granddad said. "They don't allow grandeur here."

They continued to walk down the cobblestone street. It was lined on both sides by shops, hovels, tents, and mini-villas. It was mostly populated by people of the old Roman times, but occasionally Tim would see people of a different era. They passed an olive oil shop, and Tim saw a Victorian lady passionately kissing a Roman legionnaire.

"That's not encouraged," granddad said. "But it's not discouraged either." He was staring at them as we passed.

"The kissing, or the mixed times?" Tim asked.

"Oh, the different eras becoming involved," Granddad said, and then winked. "Kissing is okay between mutually consenting entities."

Tim started laughing at Granddad's political correctness. The wink had sealed it. Granddad was not known for his political correctness. Maybe in his youth, but he had held fast to his beliefs, and did not change them when the world did. He was also champion of the understatement. As a Marine in World War II, he had fought in the Pacific theater. When asked about his exploits he would simply say that they all had done their duty. If pressed further he would say that he got to return home, the glory should go to those that didn't. IF you really pressed, and you had to be family or friend to get away with that, he would say that he got the better end of the deal. Then he would wink, and ask if you had seen his wife, followed by a hubba-hubba. Tim got the distinct impression that Granddad and Grandma did a lot of mutual consenting kissing in this Land of REM.

They turned down a side street onto a dirt road.

"Here is one you'll love Tim," Granddad said. "It's the wild wild west."

Tim did not think that he could be anymore thunderstruck than he was, but he was wrong.

"That's the Oriental Saloon," Tim gasped.

"The one and only," Granddad said. "Well, maybe not the only. You still a big Doc Holliday fan?"

"You bettcha, Granddad," Tim said in his nine-year-old voice. "Is he here?"

Granddad closed his eyes tight for a moment, and then said, "Yes, but we don't have time for him now. We have to see Grandma. The clock is ticking."

Tim looked at him quizzically.

"Not in our world, but in yours," he said. He squeezed Tim's hand, and they took off at a faster pace.

# Grandma

Granddad led the way down a vaguely familiar winding street to a house Tim instantly recognized from his childhood. It was his grandparents' two story Newport townhouse. Grandma stood on the front porch smiling. She wiped her hands on her apron.

"Timmy," Grandma said. "Welcome to the *Land of REM*. I'm glad you are here under such pleasant conditions. Please come in. You know your way around."

As Tim ran up the steps he noticed his perception had changed. He appeared physically as if he were nine years old. He stopped at the top of the steps, and as he contemplated what had happened, he physically changed to his adult self.

"It don't matter what you look like," Grandma said. "I love you, the real Timmy."

Tim ran up and gave her a hug. They were both crying now. Tim noticed that Grandma was much younger than she had been when he had last seen her. She had died at age eighty-seven, but now she appeared to be in her mid-fifties. Granddad was even younger too. He changed from the gate. Granddad noticed his quizzical look.

"We are spiritual beings," he said. "We take physical form because it makes it easier for us to exist. Your Grandma and I are happy at this age. It was about the time you were born. A very good time in our lives, mature but not too old to restrict us from doing what we want to do. We normally take this form. We can even eat and drink, although there is no physical need to."

"Timmy," Grandma said. "Would you like some pie and a cup of coffee? I just made the pie this morning. It's your favorite, cherry."

"Yes, thanks Grandma," Tim said. He was starting to tear up again. He had sure missed Grandma's cooking. It had sustained him through college.

Grandma fixed Tim a large slice of cherry pie and poured him a steaming cup of hot coffee. She poured the coffee in his favorite mug. He had not felt this peaceful and content in decades. Everything tasted great, and for now he just enjoyed the moment. They visited for hours.

Granddad suddenly changed from calm to anxious.

"Tim," he said. "You are here on a mission, and time is not unlimited."

"I understand, Granddad," Tim said. "It's just that my priorities have changed. This place is so wonderful."

"I know," Grandma said giving me a tender smile and reaching over and touching my arm. "We enjoy your company. It is a treat for us to visit with you. But Granddad is right. You are here on a mission, and you have got to watch your time here. Earth time continues on."

"We love you Tim," Granddad said. "But it's not your time to be here yet. There are still some things you must take care of on Earth."

Sighing Tim asked, "Do you know where I can find Marvin?"

'He is still mortal," Grandma said. "You will be able to feel his essence. Just concentrate on him, his life force, and you will be drawn to him."

Tim closed his eyes, and thought of Marvin. He thought of him as he had seen him that first meeting in the portal, and he thought of him as he had seen him in the hospital bed. Suddenly it was as if Tim remembered where he lived. He just knew where to go and how to get there.

"Complete your mission, grandson," Granddad said. "Remember time still flows. If you need help we will be here for you. But this is your mission."

"Tell him about the maps," Grandma added.

"That's right," Granddad said. If you get lost, there are maps at every intersection. You have to go back the way you came. The portal was the way in and that is the only way back. Back to your own life that is."

"He can't be reborn if he is still alive," grandma said.

"That's right," Granddad said. "The portal is your only way back. Remember to keep tabs on the time."

They said their tearful goodbyes and Tim reluctantly left. He could have stayed there for years. But, apparently, he had to find Marvin.

# Meeting with Marvin

Marvin was sitting on the front porch of an old Victorian two story house. He was wearing blue jeans, a tee shirt, and drinking out of a tea cup. He smiled as Tim entered the yard and started up the front porch steps.

Giving Tim a mock salute with his tea cup he said, "So you are the man that has been tracking me."

"Marvin Dispatcher, I presume," Tim said as he extended his hand.

He gave a short laugh. "And you must be Tim Stubbs," he said as he shook Tim's hand. "We met in the portal."

"I'm impressed," Tim said, sitting down in a chair opposite him.

"Knowledge is easy to obtain in the South Village," Marvin said. "If you are willing to learn, but a little knowledge is dangerous. You are here on a mortal mission."

"Yes I am," Tim said after a pause.

"Mortals have no business here," Marvin said. "They get a glimpse and therefore an edge, but it does no good. For with that edge comes the knowledge that the mortal world is not that important. It will take time, but you will understand."

"Ah, but your family," Tim asked.

"They will be here in a moment," Marvin said. "But now that moment will appear longer to me because of your visit. If it weren't for the fact that you are a friend of the family."

Tim was a little nervous and confused, but continued with what he thought he had to do. "I'm here to bring you back," Tim said.

Marvin looked at him for a long moment, and then said, "Yes, I must go back. I do have one more mission to complete. It's just that I really do like it here."

"But your family," Tim said. "They are very nice people. You have to go back for them."

Marvin was silent as he drank his tea. He finished it and then with a violence that surprised Tim, he smashed the mug against the wall. He rubbed his hands on his face and then looked at Tim with steadfast earnest.

"We all have our missions," Marvin said. "Yes, I am going back now." He stood, walked off the porch, and headed down the street.

"What the hell was that all about," Tim said aloud to no one in particular. Well, at least Marvin was going back. Tim thought his mission was now complete. He thought he'd visit his grandparents one more time and then head back. Tim looked down the street and saw a map at the intersection. Maybe he should check that out, he thought. He might never be here again.

# The Map

It was an old wooden thing. It stretched about ten feet by ten feet. The map was actually two maps, split down the middle. The left half was labeled, South Village, and contained a map of streets and paths labeled with names such as, *Wild West, the Empire, Iroquois*, and many names Tim could not read. On the right side of the map was labeled the *Land of REM*. It showed the South Village down at the bottom of the map.

Tim was fascinated. He thought the South Village was big, but it was small compared to the rest of the *Land of REM*. There was a North Village, which was ten times bigger than the South Village, and thousands of other towns. Some of these immediately caught his attention, like the "Faster than Light Village" and "Slower than Time Village."

Many were marked in symbols that Tim could not understand. One symbol he recognized more by location than anything else. It was a house looking object located on the outskirts of South Village. Tim assumed that it was the platform, or maybe the portal. He also noticed that there were many such symbols around the outskirts of the map. It seemed that the *Land of REM* was a very busy place with many access points.

Tim scanned the South Village side of the map. He noticed a street called "The Tombstone Gang." Being a big Doc Holliday fan, Tim thought, Doc Holliday was dead and he was in the land of the dead. Now would be my best time to visit with him, a dead person. Tim couldn't let an opportunity like this pass him by. He noticed it was about half a mile to the left, down the "Wild West Road."

Surely a couple of hours break to visit his hero, Doc Holliday, would not, could not, be wrong. Tim could always head back later. A cowboy hat appeared on his head. Tim looked down at his western wear and spurs. That was the clincher. He, like Marvin, liked this Land of REM. Tim went to the corner and headed west. It was time to meet some of his heroes.

# Doc Holliday

Tim turned down *Tombstone Gang Street*, and headed toward the largest building there, a place he recognized from his studies of that era. A small thrill went up his spine as his spurs clinked on the wooden sidewalk as he entered the swinging doors to the Oriental Saloon. He stood in the entranceway as his eyes adjusted to the dark. Several pairs of eyes looked up at him and then went back to their card games. He scanned the room and there, to his great joy, was John H. Holliday. Tim approached his table, where he was playing cards with several other cowboys.

"You must be Tim Stubbs," Doc Holliday said as he looked up from his game.

"How the hell did you know that?" Tim stammered.

"I've been here awhile," he said, looking back at his cards. "I know when someone is looking for me and I know how to find the story on them."

"Doctor Holliday, I am a big fan of yours," Tim said, extending his hand.

Doc looked at Tim for a long moment, then back at his cards, then at Tim again. Finally he set his cards down and extended his hand to accept Tim's hand shake.

"Fan eh?" Doc Holliday said. "That's thanks to that no good son of a bitch Wyatt."

"I love you too Doc," came a voice from the back of the room. "Someone had to take care of your scrawny ass when we were in the world."

Tim was grinning ear to ear. It was the legendary Wyatt Earp.

Josephine was sitting next to him. Frank Leslie was sitting at the table with them.

"I remember it differently Wyatt," Doc said. There was true affection in his voice. Then he turned to Tim.

"Well Tim, it is fate," he said. "Let's go up to the bar."

"I don't want to interrupt your card came, sir," Tim said.

"It's okay," Doc said. "Like I said, I've been here a long time. It's time to put down the cards and move on. Anyway, you're part of my future, so I might as well be neighborly with you."

They walked over to the bar and sat down on a couple of wooden stools. Tim sat there contemplating what his last statement meant while Doc ordered them a couple of whiskeys. A man looking like a younger version of Frank Leslie served them their drinks in two shot glasses.

"To the good ole days," Tim said, holding up his glass.

"To the future and all its happiness," replied Doc and downed his shot. Tim followed suit and downed his shot. The bartender refilled their glasses.

"So what is in your future, Doctor Holliday?" Tim asked.

He downed his shot and said, "At 9:11 in the morning, Texas time, on 8 November, the day I died in 1887, I am going back. I've got some more things to learn.

"Back where?" Tim asked.

"To Earth," he said. "It's the best place to learn, for me anyhow. I am going to be born, or reborn, depending on how you look at it. I've already picked out my parents."

"You're going back as a baby?" Tim asked. "Do you know what you will do with your life?"

"No," Doc said smiling. "Nobody does. That's the rules. You start over clean. It's like being in school."

"But it is so risky," Tim said. "I mean, you have already made it. You are the great Doc Holliday. Why go back? It could be dangerous. Aren't you scared?"

Doc roared with laughter. "Tim," he finally said. "I have much to learn and I have many faults. But one fault I don't have is cowardliness."

The rest of the saloon erupted into laughter and Tim started laughing himself. They sat and drank for several hours, telling Wild West stories. Tim was extremely happy. All his heroes were there, or came by shortly thereafter to share a drink. It was the best day of Tim's life. But finally Doc put an end to their celebrations.

"Tim," he said. "You had better be heading back. Remember that time continues on in the real world."

"Yes sir," Tim told him. They said their good-byes and Tim tried to stall. But it was obvious that he had outworn his welcome. Reluctantly he left the saloon and headed back up the street. He was surprisingly sober considering all the whiskey he just drank. He had felt good as he was drinking, but it was more of a placebo effect. He was stone cold sober now. Tim decided to stop at the map one last time.

# The Map Revisited

As Tim looked down at the map he became intrigued with the right hand side, the Map of REM. There were thousands of villages listed, with at least one portal for each one. There was an asterisk by *Faster than Light* and *Slower than Time*. He looked down in the legend where the asterisk was and it read, "Warning, will distort your time-space continuum."

There was a pathway up the center, with many branches, that connected all the villages. From the South Village, one had to cross into the North Village, then you could connect with the path and go anywhere in REM. There were little gates marked at many of the points on the path. There was one gate between the South and North villages. Tim looked over at the left map to find this gate.

He sucked in a deep breath; the Tombstone Gang Street was gone. He searched the whole map, it was not anywhere. Forcing himself calm, He slowly scanned the map. Tim then retraced his route with his finger. Where Tombstone Gang Street used to be was now a place called September 11$^{th}$ Victims' Street.

Tim hurried back down to where he had come. The street was now about five times bigger. He stopped a soldier on the street.

"Where is the Tombstone Gang?" Tim asked.

The soldier looked at Tim and then closed his eyes briefly, as if concentrating on something. He was in his dress green uniform and was wearing the insignia of a Colonel.

"They have moved on," he said. "You are still alive. You need to get back."

"Yes, I know," Tim said. "I just wanted to know what happened."

"We were all killed in the terrorist attacks on September eleventh," he said. "This is like a staging area for us."

"Thanks," Tim said, walking back toward the map. How very strange. This was April. Why had it taken them so long to arrive at their own street? Was it like space available thing or something? Where was this terrorist attack? Tim read the newspapers and watched CNN, why hadn't he heard of it? There were a lot of people there. It looked like thousands.

Tim stopped in front of the map. On the right side a small cross was moving down the path toward the North Village. He looked at the left side and found a route leading up to the gate. It wouldn't hurt to take a few extra minutes to explore he thought. Maybe he could even meet some alien life forms, or whatever they are called after they are dead.

Tim took his bearings and headed up the path, toward the gate and the North Village.

# Jesus

As Tim approached the gate, he saw a young man approaching from the other side. As the man came closer he started to change, metamorphism of some type, into a figure Tim had seen thousands of times in churches and religious pamphlets. Tim could see the nail holes in his hands.

"Tim," Jesus said. "We need to talk." He then put his arm around Tim's shoulder and guided him back into the South Village. They sat down on a bench that just materialized.

"Tim," Jesus began. "You have not been here for hours; you have been here for months. It is important that you go back. First off, you are going to be a father."

"What?" Tim said. His head was spinning. Tim was used to shocks by now, but this was too much, too quick. Jesus was telling him that he was in a coma and that his wife was pregnant.

"You conceived a child," Jesus said. "It happened after your first visit to the portal. She is now going to give birth in about a month. That means that you have spent about eight months in a coma."

"But," Tim said. Jesus held up his hand to silence him.

"Listen," he began again. "You need to head back now. There are important things for you to do. Most importantly, you have to raise that son of yours. Now go!" He pointed off toward the south.

Tim got up and started heading down the path. "But Jesus," Tim said. "I want to ask you about God, you, and everything else."

"Ask your clergy," was Jesus' reply.

"They know?" I shouted back.

"They haven't got a clue," Jesus said. "But we sort all that out up here. Just have a little faith and always do the best that you can."

Then Jesus disappeared. Tim started to run.

## Return Home.

Tim ran down the trail as fast as he could. He saw the meadow and let out a small cheer. Hundreds of people were walking up the path. They parted and let him through. Tim got to the platform and looked around confused.

"Over there, Tim," said some man in a hospital gown.

"Thanks," Tim said and headed for a door marked The Portal. He was beyond surprise anymore.

Tim ran down the tunnel and started the ascent up the many floors. There were some subtle changes, but Tim did not stop to explore. He was filled with a sense of urgency. He was going to be a dad. He ran faster, and was starting to feel mortal again. He was starting to feel out of breath.

Finally Tim arrived on the first floor; his level, the present, and burst through the front door. He took a big running leap, and jumped into the air.

Picking himself up off the grass, he headed back toward the house. It occurred to him that he didn't know how to leave.

*The Land of REM (Reboot)*

Dejected, he sat down at the desk. The computer prompt flashed at him.

"How do I get out of here," Tim typed.

"How did you get her?" was the typed reply.

"God I hate computers," Tim said out loud. Then he typed. "I went to sleep."

"Then go to sleep," came the reply.

Exhausted Tim went to the bedroom and collapsed on the bed. He closed his eyes.

Tim felt like something shifted in his mind. It was as if the whole universe had come unglued for a moment. When he opened his eyes, he was laying in a bed, in a hospital room. Georgia Dispatcher, holding little Reba, was at the foot of the bed looking at him. As Tim glanced to his right he saw a nurse holding a clip board. Continuing right he saw his wife sitting on a chair next to the bed. She was clutching his hand. She was smiling and crying at the same time.

"Oh Honey," Kate sobbed. "I've missed you and I love you and I just love you so much." Then she really lost it, sobbing and hugging Tim.

"I love you too, Kate," Tim said. He was smiling and crying now also. "When is our boy due and what in the hell is this about, a terrorist attack on September eleventh."

Georgia and the nurse stared in shocked silence as Tim's wife fainted and crumbled to the floor.

Reba let out a squeal and said, "I told you he was in the Land of REM."

## Hospital, Act II

Tim was forced to stay in the hospital for two weeks. Even after being in a coma for months, he was that rushed to his wife's aide, after months in a comma, before the nurse did, when Kate fainted. Even though the doctors said, as far as they could tell, he was in excellent health. But it was all good. Tim had learned to appreciate life, one moment at a time.

Tim loved telling the stories about the Land of REM. He even visited the hospital chapel every day, and confused the hell out of the pastor. It started out with Tim asking all the questions, but by the end of the first week, they were asking each other equal amounts of questions. By the end of week two the pastor was asking most of the questions.

Tim was asked to tell stories at the children's cancer ward. He readily accepted. He even met a young girl named Thalia who informed him that she had been around many times, and that she was here for inspiration for others. She leaned over and whispered in Tim's ear.

"I've been elected Mayor of the North Village," she said. "I take office in 2013."

Tim sat back in amazement. He realized that although he was one in a billion, he knew very little. Wow, he thought. There are people here that are beyond the South Village. It wasn't a species, or even planetary division. It was about knowledge. It was about the Universal truth.

That made Tim chuckle when he had his last hospital confinement visit with the pastor.

"So, all knowledge is good? There is nothing you don't want to learn?" asked the pastor.

"What about you?" Tim countered.

The pastor paused for a long moment, then said, "Well, according to the Bible, Jesus said Whoa unto those that come between me and the children. I would hope to never find out, first hand, what he meant by Whoa."

Tim's chuckle turned into a hard belly laugh, and he blurted out, "It's an adventure. Not a job, not a chore."

The pastor burst into laughter and said, "I have no clue as to what the hell you are saying, but I agree, It's all good."

When Tim was released from the hospital at noon after two weeks, most of the staff took their lunch break to see him off.

# Thanksgiving Dinner

"To Marvin," Tim said as he held up his wine glass. "A wonderful man who brought us all together, who taught me about happiness, and who I look forward to seeing again in the South Village, when my time here is done."

There were clicks of wine glasses all around and mutters of "To Marvin."

Even Reba joined the toast with her glass of fruit juice and said, "To Grandpa, who is in the Land of REM."

The Dispatchers and Tim's family had become very close since his recovery from his coma. He had told his story several hundred times, but they all still enjoyed hearing it. Tim also enjoyed hearing their side of the tale.

Marvin had come out of his coma briefly when his son Bill was there. Although previously brain dead, he spoke coherently to Bill and told him that Tim was in a coma from a drug and alcohol overdose. He even gave him Tim's hotel and room number. Bill alerted the authorities, who apparently just arrived in the nick of time. Then Marvin said his good-byes to everyone, to include Kate, and expired. The medical staff could not revive him.

Kate and Georgia had formed a strong friendship, and of course you couldn't help but fall in love with Reba. Bill and Sarah joined in the friendship and they were all best friends by the time Tim came out of his coma. After they got over their initial shock, Tim's tale brought him into the loop of friendship. The Stubbs have never been closer to another family. They even all go to the same church now.

Bill stood up and cleared his throat. "And also a toast to Little Doc," he said, brandishing his wine glass.

"Here, here," Tim said. There were clicks and mummers all around. John Holiday Stubbs, nicknamed Little Doc, was born at 9:11 AM on November eighth. After Tim had predicted his birth to the minute, everyone agreed that Tim's choice for a name was the only logical solution.

Kate came over and gave Tim a hug. Tim hugged her back and looked around the table at his friends and family. Tears started to spill out of his eyes. Tim had never been so happy. Little Doc started to cry.

"Put a western on the TV," Reba said. "He likes westerns."

Kate gave a sigh and headed over to Little Doc's bassinet. Tim started to laugh. Before long they were all laughing.

# Medical Report.

Initial Psychological Report on Coma Patient Tim Stubbs, by Doctor Michael Taylor, MD, DCP.

This is a strange case involving many unprecedented phenomena. At first this was viewed as an attempted suicide. However, extensive interviews with patient, family, and friends has caused me to reclassify this as an accidental overdose. What is interesting is the mass hysteria associated with this case.

1. The association between the Dispatcher family, another coma case in the same hospital, and the Stubbs family. Bill Dispatcher, the son of the coma patient, was allegedly warned by his comatose father that Tim Stubbs was in a coma. This information supposedly came from beyond the grave, in a place called "The Land of REM." Bill admits talking to Tim right before he checked into the motel. I suspect Bill knew more about the overdose than he let on. But the police cleared him, so I have let the matter drop.

2. The most interesting case of mind over matter, or suggestion, is in the case of Kate Stubbs. Her husband had

told her the time and date she would give birth. This information, also, supposedly from beyond the grave. Kate believed it so much that she actually gave birth at that exact time, a month after the prediction. I plan to do more follow up on this aspect.

3. The Stubbs and Dispatchers have now started attending church. Neither family was particularly religious before. This in itself is not unusual. Many times death and near death experiences will cause patients to come closer to their own mortality and seek religion as the answer. What is strange is that all members of both families profess that their chosen religion "hasn't got a clue." But they still faithfully attend each service. They claim you have to take it on faith and it will all get sorted out latter.

4. The final aspect is Tim Stubbs volunteering to take a demotion at work. He claims that it is more helpful to society to sell insurance to honestly cover people's medical needs, than to "screw them out of treatment in order to make money." Often a near death experience will cause a patient to reevaluate their life and make drastic changes.

This concludes my initial report. Follow up report, if needed, in ninety days.

## Blue Jay of Happiness

Dr. Mike Taylor hit print on his second copy of his Tim Stubbs' Initial Psychological Report. He dropped the first one in the shredder because it had been messed up when he spilled coffee all over it. He also had to go to his locker and change clothes.

It was a damn strange thing, he thought as he changed his clothes. Already he was beginning to believe that he had imaged the whole incident. He had been sitting at his desk reviewing the report and drinking a cup of coffee. He was taking a sip when he looked out the window. There sat a blue jay, looking at him. Then the blue jay winked, and that is when he spilled his coffee.

The End

# Epilogue

(This time I mean it)

Doctors Eugene Aserinsky and Nathaniel Kleitman were having a beer at their favorite pub, the "Gangsta," located on the most northern end of campus at the University of Chicago. It was somewhat of a celebration. They had just come from the sleep lab where they had made a great discovery. It was the beginning of the fall semester, and they had no shortages of subjects at the very generous price of ten dollars a night. The Korean War had just ended. School matriculation was at the highest it had ever been. The pub was surprisingly empty. You could hold a conversation without shouting. Basically, life was good.

"This is an incredible discovery," Dr. Aserinsky said, lifting his beer to his mouth. "We have put sleep science on the map."

"Gene," Dr. Kleitman said. "To the sleep sciences." They bumped glasses in a toast and took a large sip of beer.

"To the sleep sciences," Gene said. He finished his beer. "Another one Nate?" Nate nodded. Gene caught the eye of the waitress and held up two fingers.

"So how was Tibet? Besides being a lot colder than Chicago was this summer," Nate asked. The waitress arrived with two more draft beers.

"It was great Nate," Gene said. "I got to spend a lot of time with my great grandma Rem. She spells it R,E,M, but it's pronounced rim, like a tire rim. She is one hundred and two. That was probably the last time I will get to see her. The Sherpas are an interesting culture. They are a patriarchal society, but they have a sub matriarchal society. Kind of a separate but equal type of thing." They both chuckled. "Great grandma Rem is the spiritual leader of the Sherpas." They both sat there in silence for a few minutes. Slowly drinking their beers.

"It's incredible," beamed Nate. "I always assumed that the body went practically dormant as you went deeper and deeper into sleep, but it was the opposite. Brain function increased and the eyes. They were darting around under their eyelids like they were in some very intense action."

"I know," said Gene. "And in all five test subjects. This was not an isolated case. I think we are on to something here. In a synchronistic way it kind of ties in with a story Granny Rem told me this summer."

"Yes," Nate said. "I'm a big Dr. Carl Jung fan also. So, let's hear this story."

Gene took another sip of beer and set the half full glass on the table. "In Sherpa society Rem is a title to denote the matriarch of the peoples. According to legend the first mother of all humans was called Rem. It is the equivalent to our Eve. However, the story is a little different than the way it is told in Genesis."

"I am officially fascinated," said Nate. "Please continue."

"Well," Gene began. "To caveat the story, the Sherpas believe that when you die you go to the Land of Rem. You may also enter this place when you are unconscious or heavily asleep. The story, according to legend, has been passed down from the first Mother Rem to the current Mother Rem, my great grandma."

"I wonder if our lab rats are in the Land of Rem," Nate said. He held up two fingers to the waitress indicating another round.

"Could be," chuckled Gene. "It's a fascinating story. Granny Rem told me that the first family of humans, way before historical time, were traveling across a pasture, when a sudden and violent thunderstorm hit them. Mother Rem, the spiritual leader, took charge and was leading the tribe to safety from the thunder god when she was struck by lightning. The tribe was temporarily blinded by the flash of lightning. When their vision returned, Mother Rem was lying on the ground. A snow leopard had mysteriously appeared next to her still form. The tribe started yelling and throwing rocks at the snow leopard. It was dazed, probably because of the lightning strike. It staggered off a few paces and collapsed on the ground. They checked Mother Rem and she was dead. Her breath had left her body. The tribe formed a barrier between the collapsed snow leopard and Mother Rem. As they looked into the snow leopard's eyes they were amazed at the similarity to Mother Rem's eyes. The snow leopard took about an hour to die. When it finally closed its eyes and took its last breath, Mother Rem came back to life. She was disoriented at first, but as time passed, she returned to her normal clear-headed self. She would regale the tribe with a story of her trip through a cave into a tunnel, and finally entering into a most wondrous land. The tribe later called this place The Land of Rem in honor of Mother Rem."

The waitress had returned with their beers. They sat in silence for a few minutes contemplating the story. Nate broke the silence. "I love it! Let's walk back to the lab and check on our sleeping guinea pigs."

"I wonder if they are still in the Land of Rem?" Nate finished his beer before continuing. "What are we going to call this thing? Stage Four sleep, increased brain activity, with irregular heartbeat and blood pressure plus eyes rapidly darting around under closed lids?"

Gene thought for a moment. "Let's call it Stage Four sleep, Rapid Eye Movement, you know REM sleep."

"I love it." Gushed Nate.

Author's note; This epilogue takes place in September of 1953. That was long before the story of the Land of REM occurs. Technically it's a prologue. However, it comes at the end of the book. As my time traveling friends well know, the trouble with deviating from the forward moving linear progression of time is, there will always be problems.

# SHORT STORIES

# *Recall*

November 8th, 1956, the day my wife died for the second time. I think about her a lot. Not much else to do but think, here in the insane asylum. I also think about the first time she died. Sometimes I think about the war, the boat rides back with that crazy Indian man, and my friendship with General Douglas Macarthur. But I think more about the second time she died and that ten-year-old Japanese boy. The one I never met but whom my relationship with was probably as strong as with my wife. I have spent thirty years in this institution doing a lot of thinking, and have only recently been able to talk about it. The doctors say I should write it down and the doctors know best. I should know. I am a doctor. What is ironic is that I became a patient when I gained touch with reality. But to fully understand my story I should start at the beginning.

Elizabeth and I were born in Norfolk, Virginia, within one block and three months of each other. We were childhood friends and became romantically involved our freshman year of high school. We both attended William and Mary College and married upon graduation. That was how you did things back in the thirties. I then went to Harvard Medical School while Elizabeth got a job as a nurse at Boston General. Upon completion of my residency, we returned to our roots in Norfolk.

We opened up a small practice in Colonial Place, about a mile south of downtown Norfolk. Elizabeth was nurse, receptionist, maid and bookkeeper. I was doctor, janitor, and furniture mover. Our love and happiness must have worn off on the community. Our practice tripled that first year. That's probably why we didn't notice all the craziness going on in the rest of the world. Not until that fateful Sunday when the Japanese did a sneak attack on Pearl Harbor.

As a doctor, I was given a direct commission to Captain in the Army. Elizabeth got a job as a nurse at Norfolk Naval Base. After a few months of training to learn the Army way of medicine, I received orders to the Pacific Theater. We said our tearful goodbyes and I departed for the west coast. I would not see her again for four years and then she would be dead, for the first time.

Fate, that demon that has plagued my life, intervened early in the war. My first official duty as a doctor in Pacific Command was to treat General Douglas McArthur for an embarrassing sexually transmitted disease. My medical competence combined with my diplomacy and silence made me a "man Mac could count on."

This resulted in my being a Colonel and the Eighth Army Surgeon at the end of the war. I went everywhere with General Mac. That included the Potsdam Conferences. I gave a medical briefing on the effects of Nuclear War, and then I was free.

They said I could go home. The drawback was that the war in Europe had been over with for several months. There was only about one troop ship going back to the states every couple of weeks and most of them went to New York.

Fate intervened again and General Mac used his connections to get me on a British ship that sailed the very next day. To complete the miracle, it was sailing directly to Norfolk. Of course General Mac used his own connections on himself to fly back and would be in Norfolk about a week before me. Still, I was very happy. I wrote my last letter home that night. I knew that I would beat it home so I wrote something silly.

"Dear Elizabeth, what are you doing reading this letter? I'm back in the bedroom. Get back here. Love, Victor."

I dropped the letter in the post that morning and climbed aboard the H.M.S. Synchronicity. It was there that I meet the crazy Indian man. He was actually half British and a crewman on the ship. But he was born and raised in New Deli and I always think of him as the crazy Indian man.

We bumped into each other shortly after sailing. He stopped and stared at me, then said, "You have been blessed with understanding. I see by your aurora that you will come to understand a truth."

"Lucky me," I said and tried to move past him.

"No, not lucky," he shouted in my face as he grabbed me and shoved me up against the bulk head. He was amazingly strong for such a little fellow. "It is much better to be ignorant. Blessed is the cow who does not recognize the slaughter house."

"Okay, thanks," I said as I disengaged myself and cautiously moved away. I spent the rest of the voyage avoiding this man. I was successful, and five days later I disembarked in Norfolk.

My first indication of trouble was when I saw General Mac wearing his bad news look. There was no sign of Elizabeth.

"Victor, there has been an accident," General Mac said.

She had been running late with the indecisions of how to make herself look the most beautiful for my homecoming. To make up for lost time she had been speeding. Her front tire blew in a time prior to seat belts and air bags. There were a few broken ribs, and some cuts and bruises. But the serious injury was the brain trauma. They had drilled some holes in her head to release the pressure. But she wasn't coming around. She was brain dead. I assisted with the resuscitation and for twenty hours we kept her heart beating manually. By then General Mac had made this a top priority. We stabilized her and put her in an iron lung. But she was still brain dead. At that moment I decided to become a neurosurgeon.

General Mac pulled some strings and Elizabeth was moved to Walter Reed Hospital in Washington D.C. By then she could breathe without the iron lung. I remained on active duty and was transferred to Walter Reed with additional studies at Georgetown University. For the next ten years my life became neurology. I am not saying I never saw a sunset, or a sunrise, or had a good meal; but I will say that I never enjoyed a sunset, sunrise, or a good meal.

My theory was both brilliant and simple. Elizabeth's brain was not dead. It was not decaying. It was just not functioning. It just needed to be rewired. A modern analogy would be a computer. If the circuits get damaged, then the computer doesn't work. But the hard drive still retains the memory. Rewire the circuits and you recover the memory. If I rewired Elizabeth's brain, in a manner of speaking, then her memories, and therefore her, would come back. Regenerate the synaptic junctions and Elizabeth would come back to life.

By 1956, General Mac had fallen from grace. But by then I was fully immersed in the neurology field with many successes in both theory and on the operating table.

Not many people understood my work so the brass tended to leave me alone. My breakthrough, in Elizabeth's case, was a serum I called Brain Regeneration Fluid, or BRF. It used the B12 vitamin, which contains cobalt, as an enzyme to regenerate the electrical circuitry in the synapse. With a myelin base it basically recoats and makes functional the skeleton of the previous nervous system of the brain.

On November 8$^{th}$ 1956, I injected BRF into Elizabeth's brain. For hours I sat by her bed watching her. Then she opened her eyes and screamed.

Pandemonium ruled for the next several minutes. Elizabeth still screamed, but in Japanese. This was very disturbing since she didn't speak Japanese. Nurses and orderlies were running around getting in each other's way. I managed to grab Elizabeth and hold her tightly to my chest. I kept whispering calming, reassuring statements in her ear. I made sure I used her name with each phrase. She had been brain dead for ten years. Finally, Elizabeth calmed down. She looked at me long and hard. Then spoke, in English this time.

"Victor, what have you done? I'm not supposed to be here. I'm dead. I worked so hard. I was going to go see the giant Panda Bear tomorrow." Then she closed her eyes, fell back on the bed and died. We were unable to revive her again.

Five years after the funeral and my dark mood had not improved one bit. After Elizabeth's first death, all I had was my work. Now I had nothing. The brass covered for me and in a final attempt to revive me, they sent me on a conference to Japan. I had not been there since the war. I was linked up with a Japanese couple. A man and wife team of neurosurgeons that also chose their specialty because of a death of a loved one. I didn't pay much attention to their story at first. I just didn't care about anything. But then she said something that sent me headlong into a surrealistic world.

"What did you say?" I asked.

"I said our son just went brain dead." She repeated. "It was as if the soul had just been sucked out of him. No injury, no disease, he just quit thinking. We still haven't figured it out."

"No, before that," I said. "Something about a Panda Bear?"

"I said Miko was an honor roll student. He was top of his class and had earned a trip to the zoo to see the giant Panda Bear as his reward. He was looking forward to that trip but died the day before he was to go."

With rising horror I asked, "When did he die?"

I don't remember much after that, or even much about the following decade. There were people restraining me, a long flight in a straight jacket, lots of injections, pills, electrical shocks, and a lot of time spent in padded cells screaming. But I do clearly remember her answer.

"By western calendar, it would have been November 8$^{th}$, 1956."

AWARD WINNER

2nd Place

*The A.C. Greene Award*

Fiction 2004

## *Death Takes a Holiday*

I was dead and that was just the start of my problems. Due to several millennia of human existence, the afterlife has become as big of a bureaucratic nightmare as the mortal realm. But, thinking positively, I wouldn't be able to tell my story if it weren't. I'm also hoping that by telling my story, I will reach some of you out there who are like me and maybe we can help each other. But where should I begin? I remember taking a writing class in the twenty-first century. It taught me to start just before the crisis, so that's what I'll do. Here is my story.

I was a Texas prison guard and my wife had the annoying habit of spending more money than I could make. This caused me to seek higher paying assignments. In the Texas prison system this translates to being more hazardous assignments. That was how I found myself working the toughest wing, in the worst prison, on that hot August night.

We were conducting a *house call*. That is when we allow inmates to go from the dayroom to their individual cells and vice versa. Normally this is a slow procedure. Inmates are let out of the dayroom. The dayroom is then locked and one row of cells is then unlocked. But the inmates had been very well behaved for over a month now. I had become lazy and apathetical. I ordered the picket to open all the cell doors while I unlocked the dayroom. With hind sight I realize that well behaved inmates usually mean they are up to something. I'm sure many parents can relate to this, as this also applies to children. When the last door rolled open, there was a loud shout, and the inmates came pouring out, brandishing homemade weapons. I had a full scale riot on my hands.

Unlike in the movies, it is a Texas policy that no guns be carried into the prison. This is so that guards can't have their guns taken away from them. Therefore we can shoot into the prison but the prison, or people in the prison, can't shoot back. The drawback to this policy became clear to me as I faced fifty-two inmates armed with broken chair legs, sharpened screwdrivers, and toothbrushes with razor blades attached to them. I felt very naked with my nightstick and one pair of handcuffs. I decided that if they wanted out, then I wanted in. I headed for an empty cell with the intention of locking myself in it.

Inmate Lucifer Jones, serial number 666, was by far the meanest inmate in the entire prison system. He had ax murdered his parents when he was four, but had since moved on to more serious crimes. He also had a grudge against me. Just the week before, I had prevented him from raping another inmate. He considered this a violation of his personal recreational activities and inmate Jones lived by the feud.

An arm wrapped around my neck and I felt the sharp pain as a large screwdriver was jabbed into my back.

"Boss man," inmate Jones whispered in my ear. "This is for last week." He then shoved the screwdriver in, piercing my kidney, while he tightened his arm, crushing my windpipe. I crumpled to the floor.

I leaped up to retaliate, or maybe to escape. Much to my surprise, I discovered that my day had gone from bad to even worse. As I looked down, I saw my own body, still lying on the floor. That was when I first noticed Death. He was a skeleton looking fellow, with a hooded black robe and carried a scythe in one hand. He pointed to me with the other hand.

"Come with me," he commanded.

Apparently you have less free will after death than before it. The last thing I wanted to do was go with him. But I felt myself floating across the room toward him. We then ascended through the roof and headed up toward Saint Peter and the Pearly Gates.

Except, he doesn't go by Saint Peter anymore, he is the *Director of Admissions*. Also the Pearly Gates are not pearl but plastic and Formica. The sign over the gate read *Department of Personnel and Admissions*.

Death escorted me into the Director's office where my name was pulled up on the mainframe of life. There was my life on the screen as a flashing icon. Everyone could see that it was me.

However, in switching from windows ninety-five to ninety-eight, my social security number had been mistyped. The Director was very sorry, but I was denied admission until the problem could be solved.

Death then escorted me down to a place I had always known as Hell. However the sign over the entrance way read *Department of Rehabilitation for Souls that are Morally Challenged.* The *Director of Evil* pulled me up on his mainframe. But the whole system was connected via the web. The same problem arose. He was sorry, but, no admission until this little bug was worked out. Death had no choice but to take me back to my body. On the trip back, Death lightened up a little.

"Hey, I'm sorry, man," Death said.

I thought there were no more surprises for me that day, but then Death started to weep.

"It's always something," Death said between sobs. "They can't get anything right. I need a vacation." He went into a long, low moan and then repeated, "I desperately need a vacation"

"So take one," I said. I was starting to lighten up myself. The problems of others, always allow us to appreciate our own station in life better.

"I tried once," he said. "It's all that damn red tape."

I gave him a nod. "Go on."

"It was back in the dark ages. My wife was ragging on me. I'm married to Peace and she has got a whole lot of free time on her hands. So I decided we'd take a vacation. The world could go a week without death. I go see the Old Man and he says to submit my request in accordance with the *MFIOCITAL*.

"The what?" I interrupted.

"The *MFIOCITAL*," Death said. "It's the *Manuel for Inner Office Communications in the After Life*. We have to do this by the book up here. Anyway, I have to submit this memorandum requesting a vacation and it has to be concurred on by all the Religious and Political leaders of the day. Now, everybody agrees a week without death would be a good thing. But the egos of these guys! This is face time with the Old Man, so they all concur with comment. Now this memorandum is seven thousand pages long. The Old Man has a nana second to review it. He kicks it back with no action. There is a little sticky note attached saying that I have to address all these concerns." Death paused a moment and rubbed his boney skull. "Now this document takes up seventy-five gigabytes of hard drive and it just keeps getting worse each day." Death started weeping again.

I leaned over and gave him a big hug.

"Death, good buddy," I said. "You are trying to make the system work. What you need to do is work within the system."

"What's the difference?" Death asked.

"It appears to be a slight difference," I continued. "But it is actually the difference between success and failure. What do you want to do on your vacation?"

Death pondered this for a moment and then said, "I'd like to go fishing."

"Well," I said. "Next time you go to a ship wreck or a drowning, take your fishing pole. Then be a couple of days late getting back. Let me tell you about thankless jobs like yours. You will never get permission to do the things you want. But the boss will be quick to forgive you after the fact. It's not like there are people standing in line to take your job."

Slow understanding dawned on Death's face. We parted as friends.

The following centuries have not been kind. The only highlight was right at the start of my renewed life. I sure relished inmate Jones's look of surprise when I cold cocked him with the screwdriver he had used to stab me.

I see Death from time to time. All I have to do is walk off the roof of a building and he is right there. But the updates are always the same.

"My friend," Death said the last time we met. "We just updated to windows three billion and I can't even pull your file up anymore. It won't convert. But I'm working on it. It's a top priority."

There are thousands of books, movies, and holo-visions on vampires. You can find out where they hang out and how to kill them. Even mummies and zombies have got a culture. But I have not found anyone else like me, the misfiled undead. If you have a similar story, please contact me. Maybe we can form a support group or something.

AWARD WINNER

1st Place

*The Dr. Harry Wilmer Award*

Nonfiction 2004

## *God, The Tooth Fairy, and Everything Else*

It was the summer of 1967 and we had just moved back to Norfolk. I was ten, Steve was getting ready to start school, and Dave was a highly mobile toddler. The Cold War, Civil Rights, and the Hippie Movement, had filled the country with tension. To the three Earl boys, however, life was great, and stress free. We had just moved into a large two story house on *Newport Avenue* with an equally large fenced in back yard. Steve and Dave were making mud pies in the drive and I had climbed a tree and was tightrope walking on top of the eight-foot-tall wooden fence that surrounded the yard. I had been dwelling on a problem, as was my nature, for three days now, and decided that today I would ask Mom.

Mom was sitting at the kitchen table making meatballs. We were having spaghetti tonight, and Mom was treating us with meatballs, as opposed to meat sauce. We liked meatballs better, but this created a couple of hours' extra work on Mom's part. There is a special place in Heaven for Mother's who raise three boys. They have definitely paid their dues here on Earth. Dad was a minister, and was out saving souls and making the world a better place. We were all very proud of him, but it was Mom who got stuck dealing with our problems.

My problem had started three days ago when I had lost a tooth and secretly put it under my pillow. The next morning my tooth was still there. I voiced my displeasure concerning the tooth fairy, and my startled parents informed me that I had to tell them about the status of my teeth. Otherwise, they said, they could not ensure the tooth fairy coordination would be made properly. The Tooth Fairy may be magical, but she was not perfect. I reluctantly gave Mom my extracted tooth for safe keeping.

Part two of this drama, happened that night, when I informed Mom and Dad that the new Mad Magazine had just come out. Mad Magazine cost twenty-five cents, plus one cent sales tax. The local retail stores were very hardnosed on this. Policy dictated that the Tooth Fairy would bring me a quarter for each tooth. This meant that I would have to lose two teeth in order to buy this issue. Currently I had no more loose teeth. I could miss out on this issue.

"Besides," I said. "The Tooth Fairy, being a mythical figure, most probable did not even have to pay a sales tax. Wouldn't it be great if she brought me the Mad Magazine, instead of a quarter? It would be a little extra work on her part, but, she owed me for missing last night."

Dad had some emergency meeting to go to that night, and had to leave. Mom gave me my tooth, neatly wrapped in gauze, and I put it under my pillow. I stayed awake as long as I could, but finally

I gave into sleep. When I opened my eyes, it was morning and the new issue of Mad Magazine was under my pillow.

Now a dilemma started to brew in my brain. I had seen fairies on Walt Disney World. I knew that they were little creatures, a couple of inches tall, at the maximum. How had a fairy purchased, and delivered that magazine. I wasn't sure what mythical meant. I assumed it meant that you could bend the laws of nature; such as flying, going down chimneys, of walking through walls. I was equally sure that it didn't mean you could dispense with these laws altogether. I know that I had said, let the Tooth Fairy get the magazine. However, that was a statement out of desperation. Now that I had gotten my own way, I started to contemplate the ramifications of this incident.

"Mom," I said as I entered the kitchen through the back door.

"Yes, Jimmy," she said, not looking up from her task of rolling meatballs.

"I need to talk to you about the Tooth Fairy," I said.

"Go ahead Jimmy," she said, looking up but continuing to work.

"How did a little two-inch fairy, carry a ten by eight magazine, all the way to my house, and put it under my pillow?"

Mom stopped working. She got up and washed her hands, drying them on her apron, and sat back down. She gave me a pained look that I had seen a thousand times before. I called it the, joy of motherhood comes at a price, look. She always took motherhood seriously. I imagined she considered this question, another chore that came with the territory. Her children would love her, and she would never know loneliness.

"Jimmy," she finally said. "Do you know what mythical means?"

"Not exactly, Mom," I admitted.

"It means that they are not real," she said. "When your Dad left that night, he went to the store and bought a Mad Magazine for you. Then he snuck it under your pillow when you went to sleep."

Slow understanding dawned on me. That explained the missed night also. Of course, it had to be true. I felt a little older then. Another light bulb went off in my head.

"The Easter Bunny is mythical also?" I asked.

Mom shook her head in the affirmative. That cleared up another dilemma. I had seen bunnies at the zoo, and at shows. They appeared to be rather stupid animals. With Christianity running rampant in this country, the coordination of all those Easter baskets would take a very clever entity indeed. I just didn't think a rabbit was up to the job.

"So that is you and Dad also?" I asked.

"Yes," Mom said, a sad look on her face. "We kept the stuff for the baskets in that locked closet, under the stairway."

"Well at least Santa Clause is real," I said, giving her a big smile.

Mom shook her head in the negative. She was obviously confused.

"Mom," I whined. "Santa brings us some cool gifts. Nothing personal, but the gifts we get from you and Dad are a lot crappier than what we get from Santa."

"We give you our gifts," Mom said, a touch of irritation in her voice. "And we save the best gifts to give to you as Santa Clause."

"But Mom," I said. "The bike last year, you all gave me some clothes and a board game. Santa gave me the bike and a bunch of other really nice stuff."

"Your father put that bike together Christmas Eve, after you and your brothers had gone to bed," Mom said, her voice full of sympathy. "We kept it in the locked hall closet. No matter where we live, there is always a locked closet."

This was very strong evidence, but I was still in a state of denial.

"What about the milk and cookies?" I asked.

"Except, last year we put out wine and cheese," Mom said.

"Yeah," I said. "And that was gone too."

"It was the first Christmas after your father developed a taste for wine and cheese," Mom quietly said.

My world came crashing down. That was some strong evidence, plus Mom never lied to me. I was starting to feel very old. I sure hope growing up held no more painful surprises for me.

"Is God mythical?" I asked.

"No," Mom, the pastor's wife, said. She looked startled by the question.

"So let me get this straight," I said sarcastically. "Santa Clause, a man we can see, who brings us real toys, is mythical, but God, who is invisible, and doesn't bring us anything, is real."

Mom had a look of horror on her face. I had only seen that look a few times and it scared me. I called it her, loneliness probably wouldn't have been that bad, look.

"Jimmy," she said in a slow deliberate voice. "As far as we know, God is real. He created everything, to include the universe, this world, Dad, me, you and your brothers. This makes him very important in my book. We can't see him, but we can see evidence of him. Sometimes you just have to take things on faith."

We sat there in silence for a few minutes, staring at each other. Then Mom held her arms out for a hug and I gave her a big hug. Mom's hugs always made me feel better.

"I love you, Jimmy," she said.

"I love you too Mom," I said. "I'm going back out to play."

She gave me a tight squeeze and then released me. I headed for the back door.

"Jimmy," She called. "Keep this to yourself, please don't tell your brothers."

"Okay, Mom," I said. Who would believe me anyway? I headed out the door into the beautiful Virginia summer afternoon. Dad would be home in a few hours. Maybe I could get some intelligent answers from him.

The End (not even close).

AWARD WINNER

15th Place out of 18,000

*73rd Writers Digest Annual Competition*

Inspirational Writing

## *Angel*

This is the story of the most remarkable man I have ever met in over a decade of trucking our nation's highways. My part of the story starts in a small southern town called Bishop, Texas. I had just hooked-up to a fully loaded trailer and was having trouble raising the landing gear. I put all my weight on the handle, when the lever shifted out of gear and propelled my overweight body to the ground, with all the force of Earth's gravity. My fall was broken by a jagged piece of rock that caught me on my left knee cap. The pain was incredible, and I blacked out for a moment. I came to, face down on the ground, with a strong taste of bile in my mouth. The pain was still there. While writhing and speaking incoherently, I managed to turn over and examine my knee. I was immediately struck by two noticeable differences. First, my knee was over twice the size it normally was, and second, my knee cap was on the side of my leg, not in front where it usually was.

Truck drivers' lives are divided into two kinds of days, good days, and bad days. If you would have wagered me at that moment,

I would have bet a substantial amount of money that that day would have been a bad day. I would have lost.

A tall, lanky, middle aged hippy type, man appeared from around the front of my truck. He was dressed in typical truck driver apparel; cowboy boots, blue jeans, flannel shirt, and a black leather vest. He had long dark hair and a full salt and pepper beard. He wore a pair of ray ban sunglasses, and a red baseball cap worn backwards on his head. The image was completed by a gold cross dangling from his pierced left ear.

"Are you okay?" the stranger asked. Then as he looked at the torn bloody portion of my blue jeans with the protruding parts of raw swollen flesh he added, "No, I guess not."

"May I?" He asked. Without waiting for a reply he knelt down and grabbed my injured knee.

I started to scream out in protest, to strike him, to do anything to make him stop. But I was momentarily stopped by the sight of a brilliant whitish blue light appearing between his hands and my knee. I watched in amazement as the knee cap swiveled back into position and the swelling completely disappeared. I flexed my knee. There was no pain or stiffness. It was as if the injury never happened. I shakily got to my feet and further tested the knee. It was as good as new. Actually it felt better than new.

The stranger was walking away. I ran after him and grabbed his arm.

"Hey," I shouted. Then softened my tone and said, "I mean thank you. That was like some kind of miracle."

"Some kind of," he said and started to walk away again. I held on to his arm.

"Please," I begged. "This is extremely incredible and sort of hard for me to handle. Will you please let me buy you breakfast and maybe you can explain it to me."

He looked at my hand clutching his arm and I quickly released him.

Then he looked me in the eye and said, "No reward is necessary. The act itself is its own reward."

I held his glaze and said, "Please. I need to do this."

He contemplated for a long pause and then said, "Okay. There is that truck stop in Robstown off of highway 77. We'll meet there."

I closely followed him to the truck stop. I was afraid he would disappear. I parked next to him and we went into the little restaurant together. We grabbed a booth and he ordered a cup of coffee. I ordered the same. When the coffees arrived he began his story.

"My name is Mike," he said. "But they call me Angel. That was the nickname my daddy gave me when I was little. He said I was his little Angel. I use it as my CB handle. I have been truck driving since I was twenty-one years old. My father was a truck driver, gave the occupation some forty-two years. Before him my grandfather was a truck driver. You might say truck driving is a family tradition. It is the only thing I've ever wanted to be. When my daddy retired he gave me his truck and I became an owner operator. That was a very special day for me. My daddy reemphasized something he had been telling me since I was a little fellow. He said that us truck drivers where the 'Knights of the Highway.' We not only delivered freight but we helped people in need along the way. That was as much our job as driving. Daddy raised me right and I always lived up to that. I never went by anybody stranded on the road without stopping and helping. Even when my schedule was tight, I still stopped and rendered assistance to those that needed it."

Angel paused in his narrative, his face tightened as he recalled painful memories. He took a sip of coffee while regaining his composure.

"One day I saw an old beat up car on the side of the road with its hood up. Naturally I stopped, but as I got out and started walking to his car a young man leaped out, and started walking toward me. I asked him if I could help. In response the young man pulled a .357 magnum revolver from his jacket pocket and shot me three times in the chest."

Angel paused in his story one more time, he had a look of extreme sorrow on his face. I thought he might start to cry, but instead he took a couple of more sips of coffee, and continued.

"My world went spinning. I drifted in and out of consciousness. I remember being dragged. I remember hearing my truck start up, and drive off. I laid there for what seemed like days, although the police told me that it was only about three or four hours. Then I woke up in the hospital. One lung was punctured, four ribs shattered, with bone chips dangerously close to my heart, and a bullet fragment lodged in my spine. My insurance money was gone before I could even get out of bed. Thank God for my family. They kept my spirits up. My daddy was there every day. Finally, after about six months, I was able to leave the hospital. But it took years of painful hard work to fully recuperate. But the hard work paid off. On the fifth year anniversary of my getting shot I got my commercial driver's license back."

Angel smiled this time, "I was a truck driver again. We were returning from the Department of Motor Vehicles when daddy suggested we take a little detour. We pulled into the local truck stop and daddy pulled up to this brand new truck. Smiling he handed me a set of keys. About the same time a huge crowd of people emptied out of the truck stop and started heading our way. The whole town had turned out to see me get my new truck. They had been secretly taking up a collection for years. The truck was mine, free and clear."

Angel paused again, his eyes misty. "That's her out there. She's an old truck now, over a million miles. But I will never get rid of her."

Angel drank the rest of his coffee in silence. After about two minutes I couldn't take it any longer and blurted out, "That's a great story Angel. It really is. But that doesn't explain that thing with the lights and my knee getting fixed."

"Oh, that," Angel said. "The horror of violent crime is that it tends to victimize you twice. Once when it happens and then again when you let it affect your whole life. I was scared and mistrustful of people after the incident, especially strangers. I had been back on the road maybe a month when a similar situation arose. There was a beat up old car on the side of the road with its hood up. A young man, of about the same age and ethnic background as my shooter, leaned over the engine. I had a great urge to just drive on. To say the hell with the world because I just don't care anymore. But I knew that would be wrong. So I swallowed my fear and pulled over. Before I could get out of the truck, the young man had hopped up in the passenger side running board. He sure was a pitiful sight. I asked him when he had eaten last. He told me it had been a while since he had eaten anything. I told him to buckle up, I would give him a ride to the truck stop where I would feed him and then we would work on getting his car fixed. He was just a smiling from ear to ear. I gave him my standard introduction. You know like the one I gave you. My name is mike, but they call me Angel. He gave me a smile that would melt butter, and then said something that I will never forget. He said, 'what a coincidence, my name is Michael and I am an angel.' I gave a look up to heaven and thought, great, first one since the shooting and he's a psycho. Then I heard a ruffling of feathers, and was blinded by a brilliant bluish white light. When my sight returned there was this honest to God, halo and wings, angel sitting next to me. He informed me that I had passed a test set up in accordance with the gospel of Matthew, chapter twenty-five, verses thirty-five through forty. God was very pleased with me and had a gift for me. The angel told me that I would live a long life, free of pain and injury, and because I liked helping people so much, I now had the power to heal others. That was over ten years ago and I haven't been sick or felt pain since then. I can also heal, like I did your knee, by the laying on of hands."

I looked at him incredulously and said, "That's a really good story, but you don't expect me to believe it do you?"

For an answer he got up and walked away. When he got to the door he turned and said, "How is your knee?"

His point was well taken. I was ashamed to say that I didn't have a bible. So I bought one at the truck stop and looked up Mathew 25:35-40. Here is what it says:

*"For I was hungry and you fed me: I was thirsty and you gave me drink: I was a stranger and you took me in: I was naked and you clothed me: I was sick and you visited me: I was in prison and you came unto me. Then shall the righteous answer him saying, Lord, when were you hungry and I fed you: or thirsty and I gave you drink? When were you a stranger and I took you in? When were you naked and I clothed you? When were you sick or in prison and I came to you? And Jesus shall answer saying unto them, Verily I say unto you, inasmuch as you have done for one of the least of these my brethren, then you have done unto me."*

I couldn't help but get a little misty eyed over that. As I returned to my truck it occurred to me, today was a 'good' day.

The End

# *An Inconvenient Truth*

## (What? It's Wrong When I Say It)

The following is a work of fiction. Any resemblance to real characters, dead or alive, past or present, normal or have had a four-foot tube shoved up their ass, is purely coincidental.

On January 26, 2008, I went to Scott and White Hospital for a routine colonoscopy. My appointment was not until mid-morning, but we went in early to watch the dedication ceremony at the Intensive Care Unit. They were naming the ward after some Olympic Gold Medalist skier.[1] For two days prior I had nothing to eat, but a bottle of laxatives. I was reminiscing about my Ranger days. Yes, we could scale mountains, and take out enemy strong holds, but we never figured out how to deliver breakfast in the field. Tammy, my supportive and giggling wife was right by my side. She kept saying that now I was going to get my come upends, and then she would burst into a fit of giggling.[2]

We arrived at the operating room on time,[3] and I was given drugs. This is a good thing, when legal, and you don't have to operate heavy equipment. I was wheeled into the arena. Scott and White has a cost saving policy of selling tickets to all operations. It is also televised.[4] College football did not start for another four hours, so the theater was packed.

I don't know if it were the drugs, or I'm just nostalgic by nature, but I found myself reminiscing about the interior decorating convention in San Francisco, that I went to last year. My revelry was interrupted by shouts and gasps.

"We have a polyp," yelled Doctor Sears. I flashed back to freshmen biology. A polyp was some kind of plant. But how did it get up there?[5]

"Zap"

"We got it," laughed Doctor Sears. There was celebration, and high fiving all over the place. Even the hot dog vendors and beer vendors stopped for a moment to cherish the victory.

Next thing I know, I'm in "recovery." Doctor Sears enters. She was professional, friendly, and smelled very nice. These are amazing attributes for someone whose work area is inside sick people's rectums.

"Mr. Earl," she said, extending her hand. For narrow minded and selfish reasons, I did not shake it. "We removed a polyp." I made a mental note to never eat salads again. "I sent it to Biopsy, and we should have the results in a couple of weeks. If it is cancer, I will call you." The dreaded "C" word, hated by Caucasians as much as the "N" word is hated by black people.

After a couple of weeks, I started to relax. Then I got the call.

"Mr. Earl," a soft voice said. "This is Doctor Sears. Remember me?" How could I forget?[6] She had been intimate with me in ways even my wife hadn't. I was hoping she was calling for a second date, but as luck would have it, this was not the case.

"Yes," I meekly mumbled.

"I have good news and bad news," she said.

"I have had a very bad day, give me the good news first," I said.

There was a pause, and then she said, "I lied. There is only bad news." Another pause. "Scott and White, in a cost saving spirit, is randomly denying claims. Your claim for the colonoscopy has been randomly denied. You owe us fifteen thousand dollars. Also, your biopsy is back, and it is cancer. I give you less than six months to live. I will now transfer you to accounting where you can make arrangements to pay of your debt in the remaining time you have left."

I was put on hold. After about three hours, a rough voice comes on the line.

"Mr. Earl, this is Mr. Smith, the senior finance officer for Scott and White," he said. "I understand your health issues. Do you have a savings account or can you mortgage your home?"

"No," I said.

"Well, you can make payments of three thousand dollars a month," he continued. "Is this doable for you? When can I get your first payment?"

Like I said, I was having a very bad day. I just lost it. "You can take your payments and have a colonoscopy with them. Even if I make the minimum payments on everything else, it would take me over a year to pay of that debt. Besides, I'm not sure I picked the right denomination of Christianity. I could end up in hell.[7] Then I would really owe money."

"Now just calm down," Mr. Smith said. "Let me see what I can work out. Let me make a few phone calls." I was put on hold. This time for fifteen hours.

"Mr. Earl," Mr. Smith said. "Sorry to keep you waiting so long, but my shift ended. I've got some great news for you. Please hold. This time I was only on hold for twenty minutes.

"Mr. Earl," it was Doctor Sears. "Mr. Smith has informed me of your financial situation. I've got great news. I've agreed to give you eighteen months to live."

I breathed a sigh of relief. "Thank you," I said.[8]

Time has passed, and I was able to make a couple of payments. Then the weather in Central Texas got real screwy. I'm beginning to think Al Gore is right about this global warming thing. I am curious, about how a man who has devoted his whole life to stopping global warming, could spend eight years as the Vice-President,[9] and never mention it. Then it occurred to me, it is because the Vice-President is extremely busy.[10] Anyway, to make a short story long, because of the weather, I lost several key contracts. I went from making a couple of thousand a week to barely making ends meet. I had to meet with the Board at Scott and White Hospital. I signed a contract, and agreed to pay 28 % APR. I have a thirty year note. The good news spin off is that the Doctors have now given me a clean bill of health, and say I will live to be one hundred, pending a change in my financial status.

## FOOTNOTES

1. Peekaboo I. C. U.
2. Apparently this is a veiled reference to anal sex. A practice enjoyed by women and gay men, but not appreciated by real men, such as myself.
3. I'm not going to start telling the truth now.
4. Blacked out locally, of course.
5. I had always suspected that salads were actually bad for you. This seems to confirm that suspicion.
6. Rhetorical and somewhat sarcastic.
7. Theologians violently disagree on spiritual matters. Nobody knows who or what God is. However, all theologians agree on one issue. If there is a hell, it is well staffed by employees of credit card companies and collection agencies.
8. Special footnote to my children and grandchildren: If you are up front and honest, and willing to work things out, you can meet your financial obligations. Don't hide from them, embrace them.
9. It is argued that Bill Clinton was the "Vice" President, but that is under definition number two (Webster's Dictionary). See President Clinton's Autobiography "The Johnson Years."
10. Point of Fact: The Vice-President is so busy, that when he goes hunting, he does not have the time to identify what he is shooting at before he pulls the trigger.
11. There is no footnote eleven, dummy.

## *Fishing on Belton Lake with John Wesley Hardin*

It's Halloween where I live in Windmill Farms. This year we are actually conducting Trick or Treat rituals on 31 October even though it falls on a Thursday. Windmill Farms has a volunteer policy where you can participate as a candy giver or not, depending on your own personal beliefs. My wife enjoys this tremendously. She suits up in her Eeyore costume and sets up her card table station. This includes a battery operated Hogswart talking hat, ghostly holograms, spooky music, and of course lots of candy,

I on the other hand am not a big fan. I take the car, giving her more driveway room, and head out to my favorite fishing spot on Belton Lake. It is very secluded, but on Halloween Eve it is completely deserted. Just the way I like it. I set up my chair, put my thermos and tackle box on the ground beside me, bait my hook, and pour myself a cup of coffee in my lucky insulated tumbler. Now completely set I cast my line and sit back in blissful contemplation of the meaning of life, love, and everything else.

I am hunting for catfish, bottom feeders, so I do not have a bobber. My hook and sinker are sitting on the bottom. After about thirty minutes I get a slight tug on the line. I yank the line to set the hook, and began to reel it in. It wouldn't budge. I hadn't caught a fish. I was snagged on something. Getting up, I cautiously reeled my line in. No sense losing a three-dollar rig. As I brought it up to the shore, I saw what looked like a chicken bone. I was curious. Getting my flashlight from the tackle box I washed all the mud and goop of my catch. As I did it fell into three separate pieces. Examining it closer, to my shock, I discovered that I had caught human phalanges. I cleaned it off thoroughly and put the three fragments in my chair's other cup holder. What a story this would make. Halloween Eve and I caught a skeleton's finger.

As I was re-baiting my hook my attention was drawn to a cowboy hat floating on the water. As I watched, a head emerged under the hat, followed by a neck and smartly dressed torso. I continued to watch in horror as a man emerged from the water and stepped onto the shore.

"Hi," the mysteriously dry stranger said to me as he extended his right hand. "Names John Wesley Hardin, but friends call me Wes. I'm a lawyer and a gun fighter. Please to make your acquaintance."

"Hi," I replied instinctively shaking his hand. I noticed he was missing his right index finger. "My name is James Samuel Earl, but friends call me Jimbo. I'm a writer. Would you like a cup of coffee?" Lame I know, but I was completely unprepared for this situation.

"Thank you, sir," replied Wes. "That would be much appreciated. I got a slight chill on. A writer eh, I wrote a book myself."

"I know," I replied. "I read it."

"How could you have read it?" He asked, looking at me quizzically. I've only shown it to a handful of people."

"That's right," I replied, as I handed him my thermos top cup full of coffee. "It wasn't published until after your death. Which brings up a question, I've been to your grave in El Paso. What the hell are you doing at the bottom of Belton Lake?"

"Light weight," he responded as he took the coffee, quizzically lifting it up and down. "Well, the last thing I remember was getting drunk in a bar in El Paso when I got this searing pain in the back of my head. Then all the lights went out, and now I'm here. Where and when is here? I've never heard of Belton Lake."

"Well," I said, pausing as my mind raced. "To start with the year is 2024. You were killed in the spring of 1895 at the age of 42. Not bad for a Wild West gun fighter. Let's see, that was one hundred and twenty-five years ago. Belton Lake did not come into existence until 1954, over half a century after your death. I'm not sure why you would be here. I'm a Methodist, and that kind of theological dogma is not discussed or even considered in our circle. I've been to your grave in El Paso. It's kind of cool. You have a cage over your grave site. Someone must have thought you might escape." I smiled at this and then continued, "There is some controversy. Maybe your body was stolen and buried somewhere else. I'm not a native Texan. I came here as an adult with the US Army."

"A damn Yankee Republican," Wes scowled. "Sad, I guess we are still occupied by Federal troops, and you haven't given us our slaves back. I was sure the Democrats would rise again. I'm glad we killed that bastard, Abraham Lincoln." He threw the coffee cup that I had given him, which was still half full, at my feet. The gun fighter appeared angry.

I realized the precarious situation I was in. He was armed with a couple of revolvers, and that's just the ones I could see. I was completely unarmed, but he was missing his trigger finger. The deciding factor was that he was dead, and I could be killed. I chose my next words carefully. "Well.... the Republicans are still a major power in our country, but we are currently under a Democrat President. We are a united country. I was stationed here at the Army Fort Hood, named after the great General John Bell Hood. We are now one nation under God." I paused, holding my breath.

"Humph," Wes grunted while he stroked his clean-shaven chin. "No matter to me anyway. I'm dead. Might as well make my peace." After a reflective pause he continued, "So where is this place?"

"We are about thirty miles south of Waco," I said. I remembered that Belton Lake was constructed over a town or two. Pulling out my cell phone, I googled it. "Know anybody in Sparta?"

"Well, I'll be damned," he said. A slow smile crossed his face. "My second wife Calley had family there. My girlfriend Beulah had a half-brother there." His demeanor became agitated. "No impropriates or infidelities there. Calley and I only stayed together for about a week. I didn't meet Beulah until years later." His look became quizzical. "I always thought it was a strange twist of fate that they both had family there." He looked knowingly at me, "Where is Sparta?"

I tapped it into my GPS app and pointed, "About a hundred yards over there at the bottom of the Lake. It's very close to where I pulled up a human finger bone."

"God's world," he said. "That black book you keep tapping. I notice it lights up. It produces its own light, like nothing I've seen before. Is that a bible?"

"Ah…, we call it a cell phone," I said. "But it does possess some higher powers than what you had in your time."

"My time is done," he said with a resigned to fate tone. "Let me rest in peace. However, I believe you now have something that belongs to me?"

"I think I do," I said with acceptance also. The trigger finger of gun fighter John Wesley Hardin would be a nice artifact to own. I walked over to my chair to get it. "Do you mind if I asked you a few questions?" I handed him his bones back.

Gun fighter, convict, and lawyer John Wesley Hardin took the bones from my hand and grasped them against his right hand with his left hand. A few seconds later he released his clutch on himself, and his finger was back on his hand. "I'm tired," he said "But thank you. Pick your best two questions and I will answer them." He remained standing. He was flexing his right hand as if he had a cramp.

"Thank you," I replied. "Well first off, how many people did you kill? Estimates run from 15 low end to 60-100 high end. What's your count?"

"40," Wes said chuckling. "What's funny is that it's not the same 40 that people know about. I was in a bit of a fix and riding out of trouble. We stopped at this boarding house, well more like a farm ranch, but they took in borders that traveled that trail. It was in Labette County, Kansas in the summer of 1871. I believe they called themselves the Bender family. A very strange husband and wife with a couple of kids, they immediately put me on my guard. So, they serve dinner and my back's turned to the window which is closed over with this thick carpet. I could see the outline of the oldest boy, a strapping young man, and he's holding an axe, I can see the outline through the curtain. Well, he attacks me, and I end up having to kill the whole family. They were a crazy bunch. I don't think I was their first time they tried to kill anyone, but I was their last."

He chuckled to himself as he stroked his chin. "I never shot a man for snoring. That's pure fabrication," he said. "The rest, to include those in Mexico are pretty much as I reported them in my manuscript." He turned to leave.

"One more question, please sir?" I asked him, halting him from his movement back to the water. "You killed your first man, an ex-slave before you were fifteen. According to your own statements, and collaborated in your manuscript, this was completely self-defense. He attacked you with a large walking stick and a knife. Is this true?"

"Well," he said with a smile. "I guess that now that I'm dead, it doesn't much matter anymore." He' hesitated for a moment, then continued. "Mage was his name. a rather uppity darkie. He gave my uncle a lot of grief. So, my uncle gave me twenty dollars to kill him. ALL the judges were carpet-bagging Yankees then, so I misrepresented the story. I personally didn't want to go to the gallows."

Wes noticed I was staring at him in horror. Laughing he said, 'I suppose murder for hire is just something not done in your time."

I was confused, but then I understood. "No," I said smiling myself. "Murder for hire is still a thing, and probably not looked down upon any more than in your day. It was your terminology that shocked me. First off, the term uppity is no longer part of our language. The closest word we have for that would be defiant, and that is almost always termed in reference to white people. Also, the word darkie is an obsolete saying. People of black skin are called African Americans now."

"Like I said, "Wes stated rather matter of factly. "It's not my time anymore." He then, rather defiantly turned and walked in to the Lake. When he got to about waist deep, he gave me a dismissive wave with his right hand and continued into the water.

As I watched his head disappear beneath the surface, I came to the conclusion that I no longer wanted to go fishing. I headed home and did an Ancestry.com search. According to the Sparta, Texas 1890 census there were forty people living there. That's the number of people that Wes claimed to have killed.

## The Professor

Thirteen-year-old Brandon Hale stood outside the window, in the cold Rochester air. He looked in at the old Jew bitch. The cold only added to his rage, and it was damn cold. Even for upper New York. It was eight o'clock on Halloween night, and the temperature had already dropped well below freezing. The old biddy didn't even have trick or treat stuff up, as if she were too good to participate in the sacred tradition of giving kids candy. Well then, no treat, then a trick, and he had a great trick for her.

Brandon was certain she was the one that had squealed on him. Someone had squealed on him, and it sure wasn't Tom, his best friend. Besides, those Jews were always squealing on regular folks. She was supposedly a Holocaust victim. Tom's cool older brother, Jim, had told Brandon that there was no Holocaust. It was just a cheap Jew conspiracy to gain sympathy, and to make money. Those Jews love their money more than they do us regular folks. Well tonight, old Finkelstein, that is old Frankenstein as the cool kids called her, would pay. As soon as she went up to bed, he would smash out all her windows. Brandon smiled, for the first time that night, as he thought of all that cold air, plowing in through the broken windows of her old, run down, little townhouse.

Brandon reached into his paper route bag, and pulled out one of the biscuit sized rocks. Anytime now, he thought. Inside, just like clockwork, Anna Finkelstein glanced at the clock, put down her knitting, and headed upstairs. When Brandon heard the upstairs bedroom door close, he waited ten minutes, and then heaved the rock through the downstairs window.

The glass shattered. There was some more sound of breaking glass as the rock continued on its path, and knocked over a table lamp. Grinning madly, Brandon reached for another rock, and then, everything went silent. The falling glass stayed suspended in mid-air. It was like the whole world froze in place. A cat walking down the alley stood stock still, paw raised to make the next step. A startled pigeon was suspended in mid flap, hovering, but perfectly still. Brandon whirled, as he heard a voice behind him.

"Hello, my name is Professor Emit N. Relevart," said a bearded gray haired old man in a rumpled tweed suit. "You must be Master Brandon Hale."

Brandon, in a panic, let out a shriek, turned, and sprinted into a trash can. The pain was the worst he had every felt.

"I'm here to educate you," said Professor Relevart, helping Brandon up. "My lesson was to be on history, and learning how to get along in society, but for your safety, we will take a sidebar into physics."

Brandon, dazed, was rubbing the sore spots all over the left side of his body. He no longer held thoughts of escape, but resigned himself to a meek acceptance of whatever fate this strange, powerful man held for him.

"When living in a four dimensional universe," continued the Professor. "It is imperative, that when you are suspended in time, you do not run into stationary objects. It will hurt like the dickens."

Brandon nodded, and started to cry. He couldn't stop the tears. He felt like he was six again, the last time his mom had hugged him.

"You're a good kid, deep down," said the Professor. "You just need to be educated so that you can make the right decisions in life. It is not that you will make all good ones, nobody does. I'm just trying to keep you from making really bad ones. Since nobody else has taught you, I will. You have won a scholarship, seeing as how you come from a poor family."

"We're not poor!' Shouted Brandon. "My dad is the plant foreman. He makes six figures a year."

"I meant poor spiritually, little Brandon," said the Professor, tousling Brandon's hair. "When was the last time you did, or even witnessed a good deed? When was the last time you went to church? God has an equal opportunity program. Because you live in a deprived, spiritually speaking, family, you will receive this education free of charge. Are you ready to learn?"

Brandon nodded meekly. The Professor put his arm around the boy, bowed his head, and muttered a prayer. Brandon blacked out.

***

Anna Finkelstein closed her bedroom door and sat in her favorite rocking chair, thinking about Mauthausen. She had been very reflective today and wasn't sure why. It probably was seeing that boy in the supermarket today. He was the spitting image of Brandon, but Brandon was most probably dead. Even, if by some miracle he had survived Mauthausen, he would be in his seventies now. The resemblance was uncanny.

Anna shook her head, trying to clear the memories. She hated thinking about the past. The past held only pain. She had been happy enough in early 1938. As an eighteen-year-old newlywed, she had been a proud member of her community, living in the same apartment complex as her parents, grandparents, brother, his wife, Uncle Jon, and her baby brother. She was a Hungarian Jew, but in early 1938, that didn't hold any special connotations. Less than one year later her whole world had collapsed. She and her whole family were uprooted and moved to the Theresiensfadt Ghetto. By the time she was herded off to Auschwitz, in the winter of 1942, she had witnessed the murder of her entire family. Her husband had been the last to go, and he had died of starvation. He had sacrificed most of the food he received to keep her and her baby brother alive. Starvation is a horrible and slow death to witness, and then, as if by mockery, they had grabbed up her baby brother one day, and just shot him.

Anna wept into her hands, shaking her head back and forth, and rocking rapid little half rocks. For months she had kept the past at bay. Numbness was much preferred to the pain, but that boy today, he looked so much like the boy from Mauthausen. She remembered she had been an animal when they railed her out of Auschwitz, numb, soulless, and scared. Most of that time period was a blur, thank God, but she remembered thinking on that cattle car ride that it can't get any worse. That was before Mauthausen, and Mauthausen was definitely worse.

They say the good thing about the medical experiments, and tortures at Mauthausen, was that it kept you out of that damn quarry. On little to no rations, inmates were required to dig stone out of the ground with rudimentary tools, and carry them up to the top of the quarry. This was done twenty hours a day. For fun, the guards would force inmates to line up at the top of the quarry and leap to their deaths. This rock-faced cliff was known as *Parachutists Wall*. Anna had been there a couple of weeks when she decided that a leap from the wall would be her only salvation. She had been struggling up the side of the quarry with a boulder. She sat it down, and started walking up toward *Parachutists Wall*. If the guards saw her, they would either force her to jump, or shoot her. If they did not see her in time, she would jump on her own accord. Either way, the madness would stop soon. A peace, one she had not felt in years, fell over her body as she approached the top.

Then Brandon had appeared. He was so petrified, but there was also that spark of life in him, that had been driven out of most inmates long ago. Brandon was still human, still clinging to life. Anna grabbed him, turned around, and headed down to the bottom. They had not been seen.

She remembered that Brandon could not speak a word of anything but English. They had spent six months together in that hell known as Mauthausen. He had been terrified the whole time, and had clung to her. She on the other hand had gathered strength from helping him. Once again, she had allowed herself to care about someone. Then the day before they were liberated, Brandon had just disappeared. He had disappeared as fast, and mysteriously, as he had appeared. Anna vowed never to care about anyone again, and for fifty-five years she had kept that promise.

A loud crash, followed by the sound of shattering glass, woke Anna from her reverie. Putting on her shawl, she rushed downstairs. At her age this took a couple of minutes.

"My Lord," she muttered as she noticed the rock amongst the carnage of her living room. She heard a sound outside. It sounded like a young boy crying. Anna went out to her porch.

"I'm sorry. I'm so very sorry," wailed Brandon. He was on his knees and doubled over in grief.

"Did you do that?" Anna asked. The boy just kept repeating how sorry he was. Anna stared hard at him. It was the boy from the supermarket. It was her Brandon look alike. He was obviously in great duress. Maybe it was her thoughts of this evening, or maybe she was just a crazy old lady. Anyway, against her better judgment, but in complete agreement with her heart, she opened up her arms. Brandon ran to her, and fell sobbing into her arms.

\*\*\*

Brandon was running when he left school and headed for Aunt Anna's house. He was going to play a trick on her. He grabbed her trashcan and headed around to the side of the house. Putting the trashcan up in its slot, Brandon did his best to put on his most solemn face. Looking down he headed back to the front porch.

He glanced up to see Aunt Anna looking quizzically at him. He couldn't help it, and broke into a big grin, then losing the battle completely, started laughing.

"Honor roll?" Asked Aunt Anna as she looked at the teenage boy rolling on the ground laughing.

"Straight A's," gasped Brandon between laughs. He couldn't help it. He was always so happy around her. He had also been very emotional, but in a good way, since his lesson with the professor.

"Well get up boy," said Aunt Anna. "You knew you couldn't fool me. I've already baked an apple pie to celebrate." Anna turned to go inside, and then said over her shoulder, "Did you tell your folks yet?"

"No Aunt Anna. Not yet, but I will. I get along good with them now, thanks to you." Brandon followed her into the kitchen. "Aunt Anna?"

Anna turned and looked at him. "Yes Brandon."

"I love you," Brandon said, and gave her a big hug.

"I love you to," said Anna, a little misty eyed. She had re-realized the joys of caring for someone.

\*\*\*

In a dimension humans are not familiar with, Professor Emit N. Relevart, took out his little black grade book, and opened it to the page which contained the names Anna Finkelstein, and Brandon Hale. By each name he marked an A. He then turned the page, looked at the information it contained, smiled, and closed the book. His next assignment was in Texas, in the year 1969.

## *The Professor Two*

### Sergeant Jimbo, and the Band of Love Children

Sergeant James Malone buckled his seatbelt as the Flying Tiger Jet Airplane started its final approach into San Francisco. He was returning from his tour with the Eleventh Armored Cavalry Regiment, in Vietnam. At nineteen, he had been scared to death when he received his orders sending him to Vietnam. Now, a few days passed his twenty-first birthday, there was a sense of accomplishment, coupled with a blissful calm. It wasn't that he had survived combat. That was more luck than anything else. It was more the fact that he had overcome his fears, and helped a lot of people. Not only Americans. His hand absently rubbed the Silver Star Medal on his chest. He had saved Americans also, to include his Commanding Officer in a fire fight outside of Bien Hoa. That had won him the Silver Star. There was also that crazy band of hippies. Sergeant Malone smiled. They had no business being in Vietnam. But, the medal didn't mean much to him. What made him content was his help to the Vietnamese people, specifically the Hamlet Trung Hung.

"Seat backs up," the pilot commanded over the intercom. "We are two minutes out, on final. Welcome home soldiers."

A cheer went up among the passengers. Sergeant Malone pulled his seat into the upright position. The intercom crackled for a second or two, as if keyed up, but no one was talking.

"I'm proud of you guys," continued the pilot. There was another pause. When he came back on he seemed choked up. "I'm afraid you won't receive a very warm welcome in San Francisco, but I want you to know that I respect, and appreciate all that you have done. God bless you."

Sergeant Malone smiled as he contemplated the stunned silence. It seemed strange, and also very ironic, for they had not received a warm welcome in Vietnam either. His thoughts drifted back to the Hamlet Trung Hung.

His troop had saved the Hamlet from certain destruction when they had counterattacked an ARVN raid. He had saved even more lives when he insisted that wounded Vietnamese civilians be medically evacuated, and treated. One of these was Vu Cat's mother. That was how he met Vu Cat, the eight-year-old boy, who had coined his nickname, Sergeant Jimbo. That was eight months ago, and now, just about everybody who knew him called him Sergeant Jimbo.

"Sergeant Jimbo," said Lieutenant Beckerman, tapping him on his arm. "Let's go. You are the last one on the plane. We don't want to keep those lovely American women waiting."

"Yes sir," replied Sergeant Malone as he grabbed his kit bag, and headed down the aisle in front of the waiting Lieutenant. He was in no hurry. There was nobody waiting for him here. He had a mother that lived in Peachtree City, Georgia. He would see her tomorrow. She was planning to meet his plane when he landed at Fort Benning. There was also his high school buddies, but he had changed so much since the last time he had seen them. Being with them would be awkward, to say the least. No, he was not in any hurry.

"Good luck with the rest of your life, Sergeant Jimbo," said Lieutenant Beckerman, extending his hand.

"Thank you, sir," said Sergeant Malone, shaking the Lieutenant's hand. Good luck to you too, sir." Beckerman wasn't a bad sort, as far as officers went.

"Got to go," Lieutenant Beckerman said. "Wife is waiting for me." He turned, and ran down the gangway.

***

"Where's Shank?" asked Sexy Susie. She was tired of having to mother hen these guys.

"Token up with Peace and Tommy," said Vicky in a hurt voice. "I was coming to get you to see if you wanted to join us."

Sexy let out a sigh of exasperation, and fought to maintain control. Vicky was always on the verge of tears lately, she was probably pregnant again.

"Look," said Sexy in her most soothing voice. "The fascist pig, world dominating, oppressors are landing another plane of baby killers over at the airfield in Oakland. We have to get ready for the rally. Can you take me to them?"

Vicky nodded. She was sniffling now. Sexy gave her a hug. Why can't they stay more focused? Vicky, at twenty-two, was almost two years older than her, but Sexy was the undisputed leader of the group. It seems like now all they wanted to do was get high, and Shank, the one who had recruited her, was the worst of them all now. Well, it was time to do her duties as mother hen.

"The Band of Love Children will stop oppression," chanted Sexy squeezing Vicky's hand.

"And make the world free for love," chanted Vicky. She was laughing now. That girl's mood could change more times in a minute, than she changed boyfriends in a week.

She found Shank, Peace, and Tommy stoned out of their gourds back at the pad. None of the protest signs had been made.

"Sexy Susie," said Shank as she entered their one room pad that slept all five of them. At five foot, two, and one hundred twenty pounds, she considered herself fat, not sexy. It must be her down to her ass, long blonde hair, and big tits that made her sexy. That appeared to be what the guys cared most about. It sure wasn't her keen intellect, motherly nature, and concern for world politics. Hell, they hadn't even done one letter on the protest signs.

"The signs aren't done," she said.

"Relax, Sexy," said Shank. "The world will be here tomorrow for us to save. Have a hit."

"No it won't," she snapped. "You let the ink dry on this brush." She was close to tears now, and getting mad. They didn't understand how important this was.

"Don't be uptight," cooed Shank. "Take a hit. I think you really need it."

Sexy took a small hit, and the group seemed to relax. It did make her feel a little less uptight. All was not lost. She could still make crude letters with the dried up brush. She painted all five signs herself.

***

With eight hours before his next flight, Sergeant Malone decided to take a look around in the San Francisco Bay area. Before joining the Army, he had never been out of Georgia. After Vietnam, he couldn't see enough places. He thrived of visiting different cultures. His theory was that all people had some good in them, no matter how different they may appear on the outside. He had never been to San Francisco, and the opportunity may not every present itself again.

Sergeant Malone checked his kit bag into a locker, and exited the base into the warm muggy streets. He took a deep breath, and drank in the aroma. The place was teaming with activity. His smile broadened. He loved life, and it was moments like this that heightened his since of appreciation. Look at all those people, all those different types of people, living together in peace.

He noticed a group of about five protesting hippies, carrying signs, and chanting. He gave a quick double take. They looked like the group he had saved in Vietnam. Then he chastised himself. They all look the same to me. He hated that term. It didn't matter if you were referring to the brothers, the Asians, or a group of freedom loving hippies, the term was still hateful. He felt ashamed, but still, they looked so familiar. Sergeant Malone decided he had to get a closer look.

"The Band of Love Children will stop oppression," chanted the young lady with long blonde hair. She did look like Susan, and her voice was similar. Only this girl's voice was harsher, and more forceful.

"And free the world for love," replied the other four in the group.

Sergeant Malone approached staring quizzically, his smile frozen on his face. The leader of the group spun around, and glared at him. The sign she was carrying had the words Baby Killer crudely painted in bold black letters. Her face was contorted in rage.

"Baby killer!" she screamed at him. She then bent down, and picked up a paper cup. With one deft motion, she threw its contents, hitting him squarely on the medals on his chest. It splashed up into his face, and he was bombarded with a strong urine smell.

"Get the baby killers out of Vietnam," she spoke directly at him. Her voice was choked with hatred, and rage. She lifted her sign up over her head.

"Get the baby killers out of Vietnam," she said again, and proceeded to bring the sign down on top of his head. The others were chanting behind her.

Sergeant Malone lost it. He had not cried his whole time in Vietnam, but all this hatred and rage on such a peaceful street overwhelmed him. A whole year's worth of grief came bubbling out, and he began to sob. They were deep soul wrenching sobs that he couldn't control. He couldn't even make an effort to ward of the blow.

The blow never came. After a moment he looked up. She was frozen in front of him. Her face was a mask of rage, but unmoving. Disbelievingly he looked around. Everybody was frozen still. Make that everything, for the cars, buses, trucks, birds, cats, and even a windswept newspaper were frozen stock still. Nothing was moving. Had he lost his mind?

Movement caught his eye, and he turned to see a bearded gray haired old man in a crumpled tweed suit approaching him. He was carrying a towel, and a steaming mug.

"Sergeant Jimbo," he said, affection in his voice. He handed Malone the towel. "Clean yourself off."

Sergeant Malone took the towel, and started to dry his face. Everywhere the towel touched instantly became clean. It even got rid of his five o'clock shadow, and polished his medals.

"For you," said the man. He handed him the mug, and took back the towel. "French vanilla coffee, with one cream. I believe that is your favorite. Just the way your mom makes it."

"How did you know that?" asked Malone.

The man broke into a hearty laugh. "I love you mortals," he said. He gave Malone a hug. "I just froze time, and handed you a magic towel, but your concern is how I knew what your favorite coffee was."

Malone started to laugh too, although his was border line hysteria.

"My name is Professor Emit N. Relevart. I work for God. It's kind of an angel thing. I help people that are on that point of singularity where their lives can go in one of several directions."

"And my life is at that," Malone paused for a moment. "Point of singularity?"

"No, no, my boy," said the Professor. I just wanted to say hi, and cheer you up a bit. My business is with your friends, well specifically Susan. You'll do fine in life. Sure, you will make mistakes, and there will definitely be those hard times, but you'll handle things okay, albeit imperfectly."

"What do I do?" asked Sergeant Malone. He was calming down now.

"Just have a seat over there, and relax." The Professor hesitated a moment. "I appreciated what you did in Vietnam. You helped a lot of people. Not all soldiers are like you." He gave a smile. "When you finish your coffee, the world will go back to normal. Movement will return. I'm afraid I'll have to take my mug back, it will disappear on you."

Malone nodded.

"Goodbye, Sergeant Jimbo," said the Professor extending his hand. "I hope you will maintain your positive outlook on life."

He then disappeared. Sergeant Malone looked around for a brief moment, and then headed to the bench the Professor had indicated. Sitting down he began to drink his coffee. It was as good as mom's.

***

Sexy Susie had just thrown a cup of piss on the baby killer. He had the nerve to smile at her while wearing a uniform full of stripes and medals. It was the last straw on a stress filled day, and it put her into a rage. How dare he approach her like that, as if they were friends. He probably wanted to rape her. She was going to beat him in the head with her sign. She lifted it up to hit him. She could hear the others chanting behind her. They were in the spirit of it now.

"Get the baby killers out of Vietnam," she said, as she brought the sign down on top of his head.

He was gone. He just disappeared. The world was spinning. Now they were in the woods somewhere. Some type of jungle. Maybe she shouldn't have taken that hit of Shank's pipe after all. No telling what was in it.

"What the hell?" She heard Shank's voice behind her.

Vicky began to cry. "Where are we?"

Peace and Tommy walked in front of her, their eyes wide.

"Far out," said Peace. She squeezed Tommy's hand. They walked off down the trail in front of her.

"This is a good trip," said Tommy. He and Peace intently watched a monkey skitter across some upper branches.

Sexy managed to round them all up about the time a small oriental boy came running down the trail. He stopped when he saw them, and shouted something in a foreign language. It sounded like, "Have a coke with Robert E. Lee." That didn't make any sense. What had Shank given them.

The small boy was talking again. "Americans?"

Sexy nodded. Oh, God, she thought, get me out of this trip. Sexy always hated being stoned. This had come on so suddenly. One moment she was okay, bashing in the head of some baby killer, and the next she was in a jungle talking to a small oriental boy.

"You come, bad guys on the way," the boy was saying. He was tugging at her arm now. "Quickly, Charlie almost here."

She was dizzy, but slowly starting to understand. They were in Vietnam. Someway, somehow, they had been transported to Vietnam. Maybe God was giving them a chance to bring peace to this war torn country.

"It's okay," she said to the boy, then turning to the group.

"Come on Band of Love Children, we have a mission from God."

They starred at her as if she were insane.

"Lady, you got to go now," the boy said, and started running down the trail.

"The Band of Love Children will stop oppression," she said, and held her fist up in the air. The group did not respond. They still looked at her as if she were crazy. "Follow me. We will free the world for love." She took off after the boy. The group followed.

You could hear mortar rounds landing, coming from the other direction.

As she caught up with the boy she yelled. "Stop. We can bring peace to this region. No need to run or fight."

"Lady, you crazy," was his response.

The others had caught up, stopped, and gathered around her. They were looking at her quizzically. She felt the exhilarating zeal of her mission, a mission from God. She would save the world.

"Today Vietnam, tomorrow the world," she said, and raised both arms in the air. A man wearing black pajamas appeared at the far end of the trail. She looked down the trail at him. "Don't worry my friend, we are all on the same side here. We will help you. Together, we can stop oppression."

He raised up his rifle, and shot her. It hurt really bad.

\*\*\*

Sergeant Malone slowly drank his coffee. He stared intently at the blonde haired girl, frozen in time, her sign suspended in an ark to crash down on his head. It sure looked like Susan, but that would be insane. Of course, it was no crazier than anything else that had happened today, or this whole year for that matter. His mind drifted back to Vietnam.

Vu Cat had come running up to his track. "Sergeant Jimbo! Sergeant Jimbo!" Behind him came a group of …...hippies. They were carrying a wounded girl who had been shot in the chest. Her white cotton dress was soaked in blood. "She shot!"

Sergeant Malone, track commander, and senior medic was instantly out of the track. "Set her here." They laid her next to the vehicle, and backed off. That was good. At least they wouldn't get in the way. He quickly checked her vitals. Stable, although her pulse was rapid. Her collar bone was shattered. The bullet had hit her in the upper right part of her chest. It had not only shattered her collar bone, but took off part of her shoulder. She was moaning something.

"I was trying to bring peace," she moaned. "Why did he shoot me?"

"There are no politics on the front lines," he said without thinking.

She looked up at him, and starred for a while. Finally she smiled. "It's you."

"Yep, it's me. What is your name?" He was rapidly applying first aid to her. Not really listening to her.

"Sex...," she gasped, then looked him in the eyes for a while. He felt it hard to concentrate while she was staring at him. She had very beautiful eyes. "Susan," she said.

"Well, Susan, it will be okay. You will live, although you will have a pretty nasty scar. What are you doing here?

"Trying to save the world," she gasped. "Kind of silly, isn't it?" She gazed at him with those deep blue eyes.

"Not really," he said. "That's the same reason I'm here." They starred into each other's eyes. There was a spark of understanding that passed between them.

Sergeant Malone turned to Vu Cat, and in Vietnamese said, "Ask Lieutenant Beckerman to call a dust off." Vu Cat took off toward the Hamlet Trung Hung. Malone then turned his attention to Susan, and began to comfort her.

Three hour later, Warrant Officer Steve Earl landed his Huey helicopter on LZ Bravo. Malone was waiting for him with Susan. The others had mysteriously disappeared.

"Sergeant Jimbo," the pilot Steve Earl said. "What you got for me?"

"She's been shot in the chest, sir," said Malone. "An American."

"Civilian?" Earl asked.

"Yes sir," said Malone.

"You got orders?" Earl asked, smiling.

"No sir," said Malone, looking at the ground.

"Wow," said Earl. "Didn't see that one coming. Load her up. Besides, this betters my odds." He gave Malone a wink.

Malone quickly loaded Susan into the helicopter. After she was secured he asked. "What odds are those?"

"Well," said Earl in his Texas drawl. "Half the Regiment says that Charlie will kill me before you get me court martialed. Being the intelligent man that I am, I figure, that if I'm dead, I can't collect on the bet. So I'm betting heavily on the court martial." Warrant Officer Earl pulled pitch, and the chopper rose up in the air.

Malone looked up at the chopper, smiled, and rendered a salute. He winked back, and mouthed the words, thank you.

***

Sexy Susie, or Susan, as her parents called her, passed out as the chopper lifted off. She awoke in a cloud filled world. An old gray haired bearded man in a crumpled tweed jacket was sitting next to her.

"Hello Susan," he said. "My name is Professor Emit N. Relevart. Would you like me to stop the pain?"

Susan nodded. She felt calm, and at peace.

The Professor leaned over, and touched her wound. It immediately stopped hurting. "I'm sorry you had to go through this, but I think it will be a benefit in the long run. I work for God, it's an angel type thing. Your friends, the Band of Love Children, have already been returned. Would you like me to take the scars away?"

Susan thought of the battle worn, and scarred face of Sergeant Jimbo, the man who had saved her. "No, it will help me remember."

The Professor looked at her and smiled. "I had a feeling you would say that." When he removed his hand, her wound had healed by six months. It was still a nasty red scar.

"Thank you," she said, clutching his hand.

"The privilege is mine, Madame Senator," he said. "I must now return you."

"I understand," said Susan. As she faded into unconsciousness she mouthed the words, thank you. In the next moment she was smashing her protest sign into the empty pavement where Sergeant Jimbo had been standing.

***

Sergeant Malone had finished his cup of coffee, and true to the prediction, the cup had disappeared. He looked over in the direction of the girl in time to see her smash the sign into the pavement. Her face had changed now. She was more peaceful looking. As she came up from the blow she looked around, panic stricken. She was crying like he had been. She saw him, and broke into a smile.

He made contact with those beautiful blue eyes, and had to smile back. It was Susan. What a day this had been.

"Sergeant Jimbo!" Susan screamed as she came running toward him. She caught him in a giant bear hug, and planted a giant kiss on his lips. "How can I every repay you?"

"Well," said Malone, a little off guard. "I've got six more hours here. Can you give me a tour of San Francisco?"

Taking his hand in hers she gave it a squeeze, and said, "I think I can do that soldier boy." As they walked off down the street, the Band of Love Children gave out a loud cheer.

***

Professor Emit N. Relevart took out his little black book, and turned to the page with her name on it. By her name he marked an A plus. In parenthesis, next to it, he wrote, year 2008, Susan

Malone elected to U. S. Senate. He closed the book, and put it in his pocket. He had one more stop to do today, and that was in Killeen, Texas, in the year 1984.

## *The Professor Three*
### Smoking and the Single Mom

Beth expertly wheeled through traffic using her left hand as she lit her cigarette with her right. She had three minutes to pick Karen up from school, and two hours before time to start her second job. She had done this drill every school day this year and had become quite an expert at it.

"You're so good," she said aloud as she pulled into the school lot just as the bell rang. She lit another cigarette, and let out a plume of blue gray smoke, relaxing for the first time since six o'clock this morning.

"Hi Mom," said Karen. Beth waited patiently for the ritual to unfold. Karen opened the back door of the car, put her backpack in the seat, then locked and closed the back door, and opened the front passenger door and got in. She did not say a word until her seat belt was properly fastened, and tightened, intently concentrating on every action.

"Good girl," said Beth. "How was school today?"

Karen looked up and smiled. "Fine Mom," she said. "We learned that President Regan was also a movie star when he was younger. Our teacher, Ms. Anderson laughed, and said he was still playing a movie role. We also learned to play Three Blind Mice, on the potato flute." Then her face became studious as she observed her mom take another drag off her cigarette. "We learned in Health class today that smoking is bad for you. It is unhealthy. If we know someone who smokes, we should urge them to quite. Smoking can make them sick, and they could even die from it."

Beth exhaled another plume of smoke while giving an exasperated sigh. "Sweetheart," Beth said as she batted some smoke with her hand. "That doesn't apply to single moms who have to work two jobs to make ends meet. If Mommy doesn't smoke, Mommy goes crazy. And if Mommy goes crazy, she takes a lot of people with her. Understand?"

Karen nodded. She had a quizzical expression on her face. She didn't really understand, but she knew better than to argue with that statement. "Yes Mom."

"I'm taking you to Nanny's today," Beth said as she exhaled smoke, consciously aiming for the open window. "I'll pick you up after I get off work."

Beth finished her cigarette and fought the urge to light up another cigarette. It was only five minutes to Nanny's house. She could wait to light up until Karen was gone. She pulled up behind a pickup truck at a red light.

Beth looked out her window at an Army soldier, pushing a baby stroller, his wife clinging to his arm, as they walked down the sidewalk. They were laughing and talking. It made Beth a little envious. She had often wished she had a family. A mother and father, a husband, the normal things everybody else seemed to have. She let her gaze drift behind them.

Suddenly she jerked her attention back to the soldier family. They had frozen in mid stride. Beth wheeled around wildly; everything was motionless. Karen sat staring ahead, not moving, Karen was not even breathing. Beth took her foot off the brake, and hit the accelerator, at the same time trying to turn the wheel hard to the left. Nothing moved. The brake remained motionless in the depressed position.

"Hi Bethy," said a familiar voice.

Beth turned and looked into the face of her mother. "Mom," she sobbed. Her eyes filled with tears as she thought back to the last time, she had seen her mom alive. Beth was only sixteen when her mother had finally succumbed to lung cancer. It had been a horrible year for everybody. Beth had been filled with such rage and confusion. She had dropped out of school and run away from home. A year later she found herself smoking three packs a day, and pregnant with Karen. She never regretted Karen, but life had not been easy for her after that.

"There is someone I want you to meet," said her mom. Her eyes were also full of tears. There was a bearded, gray-haired man in a crumbled tweed suit standing next to her. "This is Professor Emit N. Relevart," she said gesturing toward the strange man. "He works for God; it is kind of like an angel thing."

"Please to meet you Beth," said the Professor, extending his hand.

Beth shakily took it. "What have you done to Karen?"

The Professor smiled. "Well, technically nothing," he said. "She and the rest of the world are going through life, business as normal. You on the other hand, have been taken out of the time space continuum. That means that the world appears to be frozen, or completely still ... from your perspective. Let's take a walk, relatively speaking."

Beth found herself floating upward, next to the Professor, and her mom.

"I'm sorry sweetheart," said Beth's mom, as they floated into a cloud. "I wish I could have been a better role model."

"Mom," Beth said. She was starting to cry again. "You gave me love, and I loved you."

"Sometimes that's not enough." Beth's mom moved next to her, and they gave each other a hug. They were now completely engulfed in the clouds, but they could still see each other.

"We all have a high respect for the love in this family," said the Professor. He had moved in next to the hugging couple, and they were now standing upright within the clouds. "That is why you are given this opportunity to break this vicious cycle."

Beth's mom gave a knowing look. Beth stared at him uncomprehending.

"I am going to show you three scenes," said the Professor, touching Beth's arm. "Three events, one of which is in the past, and can't be changed, but two are in the future. They will happen if the current course goes unaltered. However, with your effort, they might have a better outcome."

The Professor gave her a compassionate look and squeezed her arm. "It will be a hard lesson, but one that if learned, will be well worth it. Are you willing to do this?"

"It is very, very important," said Beth's mom. She was crying again.

"I'm scared," said Beth. She was nodding her head in the affirmative.

The Professor gave her a smile, "A common state of being for mothers." He waved his hand, and Beth was sixteen again. She was at the hospital, visiting her mom. It was her first visit.

"Hand me my cigarettes, girl," her mom was saying. She was struggling to get out of the hospital bed. "Walk with me outside."

"Mom," whimpered Beth. "Don't you think you shouldn't smoke? I mean with your illness, and all."

"The doctors aren't really sure what causes this," Mom said, putting the cigarette in her mouth as she walked down the hall toward the atrium. "Besides, if Mommy doesn't smoke, Mommy goes crazy. And if Mommy goes crazy, she takes a lot of people with her. Understand?"

Beth didn't really understand. Why did her mom have to be sick and away from home in the hospital? Why had her dad left? Why was life so hard?

Beth watched as if she were watching a movie in fast forward mode. Except she was aware and remembered every sensation, every nuance, as it occurred. As the year and her mother's illness grew, so did her confused anger. She became mad at the world, and herself.

"I'm sorry you had to go through that," said the Professor. They were back in the clouds. Beth and her mom were both weeping.

"I'm so sorry too," said her mother. She was tightly clutching Beth.

"I needed the pain to be fresh," said the Professor. He looked like he was also hurting. "Most people have a tendency to rationalize. This makes that harder to do that. Are you ready to continue the lesson?"

Beth looked into her mother's tear-streaked eyes. Her mother nodded at her.

"Don't make the same mistake I did," her mother cried.

Beth gave her a hug, and whispered, "I love you." She then turned to the Professor and nodded her agreement.

"This is the way things are scheduled to be on the current unchanged course," said the Professor. He gave Beth a smile. "Maybe these lessons will give you the strength to change things." He gently touched Beth's arm.

Beth was at a funeral, her funeral. It was not well attended, as expected. She had not been big on, or had time for friends, but she instantly recognized one person in attendance. The crying teenage girl had to be Karen. She looked so young but carried herself so grown up. She seemed hard, and bitter, for some reason. That scared Beth. A young teenage boy walked up to her and put his arms around her. He gave her a tight squeeze. Karen reached up and stroked his head.

"Thank you, Todd, for being here," Karen said. She turned into his arms and started sobbing. "It was such a tough time, and she still lost the battle. Why do these bad things happen?"

"I know baby girl," said Todd. "Life is not fair. And what does it matter anyway?" Todd started stroking Karen's hair. She clutched him tighter, almost desperately. "When my dad died of liver cancer," Todd continued. "I thought it was the end of the world, but then I realized, we all will die. We might as well feel good in the short time provided for us. Come with me. I have something that will ease that pain." Karen tucked tightly under Todd's arm as he led her out to the parking lot.

"No," Beth groaned. The Professor changed the scene, and they were surrounded in cloud cover again. Beth's mom was weeping beside her. The Professor clutched both ladies close to him. Then Beth's mother disappeared.

"In the future, that will be your death, if you continue on your same self-destructive path," said the Professor. "It can change, at least for a little while, but the last scene I am going to show you involves the cycle, or pattern, or whatever you want to call it. It is the ramifications of actions on others because of you." The clouds started to dissipate.

Beth watched as a run-down old station wagon; she had never seen before pulled to the curb in front of a house in a section of town she recognized. This was that neighborhood in Killeen, near

Condor Park. It was built around World War II. They currently lived in that neighborhood on Metropolitan Avenue.

Karen put the car in park and shut off the engine. She turned to the back seat and spoke to her three-year-old son.

"You stay right here Tripp," Karen said. "Mommy will be back in a little while."

"You said we were going to Mickey Dees," Tripp said.

"In a little while baby," Karen said. "I have got to get some stuff. If mommy doesn't get her stuff, then mommy goes crazy. When mommy goes crazy, she takes a lot of people with her. Understand?"

Tripp nodded. He didn't really understand, but he knew not to argue with mommy when she said that. Karen pulled the car keys out of the ignition and exited the car leaving Trip inside by himself. She walked up to the door and rang the doorbell.

"Well hello Karen," said a man in casual but expensive clothes as he answered the door. "What do I owe the honor of this visit?"

"I need a couple of grams of crack," said Karen. She could see over the man's shoulder into the living room where a large group of naked people, most of them male, were engaging in various acts of partying.

"I would need cash for that," said the man.

"Come on Benny," said Karen. "You know Todd is in jail. I don't have that kind of cash. I'll have to take it out in trade."

Benny opened the door a little bit wider and ushered Karen inside. "We are doing a shoot. A classy little number called Gang Bang Girls Number 97. We could use another girl. If you do your scenes as instructed, I will give you five grams plus a couple of C notes for the rest of life's worries."

"Thank you, Benny," said Karen. She reached over and squeezed his arm. "You are a life saver." Karen entered the living room, which was also the movie set, and began to disrobe.

Three and a half hours later Karen returns to her car. She had taken a taste to get the edge off but had restrained herself from going further because she was going to take Tripp to McDonalds, and she so loved her Tripp. Karen glanced in the back and saw Tripp sleeping soundly on the back seat. She stumbled into the front seat, fished out her car keys, and started the car. Putting the car in drive, she took off down the street. About half a block down Metropolitan she side swiped a car with her passenger side.

"Whoops," Karen giggled. She was feeling pretty good. A man came out of a house and started yelling. "I'd better get out of here," Karen said. She floored the car and sped off down the road. When she got to Condor Street, she swung a left, and headed towards Condor Park, W.S. Young Drive, and the McDonalds Restaurant. She stopped at the stop sign on Zepher. A KPD patrol car, lights flashing, was headed down Zepher. He slowed and looked at her and the damaged side of her car as he went by. The police car stopped.

Karen panicked and pushed the accelerator pedal to the floorboard. She got about fifty yards down the road before plowing into the back of a dark pick-up truck. The hood of her car buckled. Antifreeze, oil, and gas leaked out into the road. Tripp, unsecured, was slammed into the back of the front seat. Karen, coming off her taste, was now scared and desperate. The Killeen Police Car now pulled in behind her, sirens blaring. The police car stopped for several minutes.

Karen had one thing that Todd had given her, one thing for sure, and that was the old Ruger thirty-eight that was in her purse. Karen, discombobulated, grabbed her purse off the floor. Struggling, she pulled the old revolver out of her purse.

"I love you Tripp," Karen said to an apparent empty back seat, and exited the station wagon while cocking the hammer of the gun. Tripp, hearing his name, started to regain consciousness, and began to move.

Officer Nix exited his cruiser and drew his gun. "Ma'am," said Nix. "We don't have to do it this way. Please put the gun down." He continued to draw a bead on Karen who was about thirty feet away, which was too far away to have a fair chance at taking her gun away from her by physical ability before she could get a shot off.

Karen approached the cop. She heard Tripp groan in the back seat. Damn, she thought. She had promised the kid a happy meal, and by God, she would get it for him. All she had to do was kill this cop.

Beth watched the scene unfold from three sides simultaneously, thanks to the Professor.

\*\*\*

KPD Officer Nix screamed, "Lady, we don't have to do it this way, please!" By regulation he was supposed to shoot center of mass, but she was just a kid, and that would probably kill her. He diverted his aim to her right shoulder blade. He would not kill this one. She raised her gun and pointed it at his head. It was a double action gun; she cocked the hammer……

Officer Nix fired his weapon.

\*\*\*

Karen just wanted to go to McDonalds. She finally had some money to spend on Tripp. The taste she had taken at the house was probably a little too strong, but now she just wanted it all to go away. Tripp was moaning, he probably had hurt himself. All she wanted was to get him to his Mickey Dees. He could have whatever he wanted. Karen loved Tripp. If she could make this cop go away, then all would be alright. Todd had taught her how to cock and shoot the gun. She pulled the hammer back and pointed it at the monster.

A sharp pain in her neck made her whelp. She pulled the trigger and fired her pistol. Then she collapsed to the ground. She saw flames all around her.

\*\*\*

Tripp heard his momma's voice and rose up from the floorboards where he had been violently thrown when the car had slammed into the back of the pickup truck. He tried to pull himself up. He managed to get one hand out the window and the other on the arm rest and heaved himself up when he heard a loud bang. His right hand, wrist snug against the rolled down window, disintegrated as the bullet slammed into it, and deflected toward his mom's neck and carotid artery. Tripp heard his mom yelp, and then heard another loud bang, and then flames were all around him. He was starting to burn.

\*\*\*

"No, no, no, no, no," screamed Beth! The Professor moved close to her, pulling her out of the scene. He wrapped his arms around her, and she collapsed weeping into his chest.

"It just takes a slight change in attitude, and the whole world will change," said the Professor. "Our impacts on the little ones are great. We need to take that seriously and with great responsibility."

Beth's weeping subsided, and she looked at the professor with fierce determination. "That scene we just saw," Beth said. "Will never, ever, ever, happen!" The Professor smiled down at her.

"You must change your attitude," said the Professor. "Forewarned of an event can prevent the event, but if the character does not change, it will just play itself out in another event. It is the outlook on life that is important. Break addictions. Enjoy life. Learn from the past, plan for the future, but live in the present. It really is as simple as that. Don't let things rule your life." The Professor paused and scratched at his scruffy beard.

"The events you just saw will not happen now," continued the Professor. "Because I have shown them to you, but equally horrific events could happen if major changes don't happen in your life.

"You are forewarned," said the Professor. "And I think this will turn out good."

\*\*\*

Beth felt the car's movement and slammed on the brakes. The car in front of her continued, moving further and further away. The driver glanced back at Beth in his rear-view mirror. The Army couple stared over at Beth's car, while the soldier moved in between them, and gently guided his family away from the stopped car. Beth collapsed against her steering wheel and began to weep.

"Mom," Karen said with real alarm in her voice. "Are you okay?" Karen, in a move that even shocked her, unbuckled her seat belt, and reached over for her mom. This only made Beth cry harder. Beth put the car in park and hugged her daughter. They were both crying now. They stayed that way for several minutes.

"I'm okay baby, and I'm going to quit smoking," Beth said. Beth hugged Karen deeply. Beth and Karen sobbed into each other. After a few minutes the moment subsided.

"It's okay mamma," said Karen. "God's will be done. Todd told me that. His father is dying of liver cancer."

Beth recoiled in horror. "You must never see this Todd again." Beth said. She pushed Karen away.

"Mom," Karen cried. "He needs me. His dad is dying. Please mom, please!"

Beth remembered what the Professor had told her about forewarned could cause one horrific event to be replaced by another equal or even more horrific event. She had to be smart here. It was not a matter of trying to outsmart the system with specifics, but a matter of learning your lesson and doing the right thing. She was, by God, Karen's mom, and even though it would be hard, she had to teach principles to her daughter. She would not use the Professor's gift to her to try to outplay specific events. That was not its purpose. Beth felt stronger than she had in a long time.

"Of course, baby," Beth said. "Todd needs you, and you are a wonderful person who helps others. I'm so sorry I snapped at you. We can overcome anything, because we face our problems head on. We are champions!"

Karen gave her mom a big hug. "I love you mom," Karen said. "We are champions!" Karen clutched her mom hard and began to cry again. Karen did not know why she was so emotional now, but something big was happening, and now she knew she was a champion who could handle it.

Beth put the car back in drive and moved away from the curb. "Let's go to work first," said Beth. "I need to talk to my boss. They are great people. They may be able to help me quit smoking. Then I will take the day off, and we will both spend time with Nanny. It will be a great day. And buckle that seat belt!"

"Yes ma'am," said Karen. She was giggling as she put her seat belt on. "It was totally delinquent of me ma'am. It won't happen again." Karen was feeling more relaxed than she had in a long time. She liked her mom's new slogan. We are champions was a lot better than; if mommy don't smoke, mommy goes crazy and takes a lot of people with her statement. Karen now had hope for a possible good future.

Beth wheeled the car into her second job at J&S Trucking. They were struggling. They didn't have the overtime to give her, but they paid her better than minimum wage, and they gave her bonuses when she made money for the company. They also took their losses without penalizing her, even when it was her fault. This was her favorite job. She truly wished this company well and hoped for a future with it.

"Hi Bill," said Beth walking into his front office. Karen was in tow. Bill Beckerman, the Truck Manager, looked up in alarm.

"Well, hi Beth. Hi Karen," said Bill, he looked very concerned. "Is everything okay? Why is Karen here?" Bill stood up. He was the nervous type. He had seen a lot of action in Vietnam, and people gave him his space. Later this would be diagnosed as PTSD, but this was 1984 and Bill was just considered high strung.

"Everything is fine Bill," said Beth. "I just need to talk to Jim or Susan. I'm going to quit smoking, and I need their help."

"Sure," said Bill. "Jimbo is in back, working on a truck. Susan is collecting a bill. She should be back in ten minutes."

"I'll talk to Jim," said Beth. Bill stepped aside and let them pass. Bill scratched Karen's head as she walked by. Karen giggled and gave him a couple of fake punches as she passed. Bill feigned injury and gave them both a huge smile. Bill really loved these two.

"Hey Jim," said Beth, entering the garage. She was nervous as hell and physically shaking. "This is complete craziness," Beth continued. She was talking fast, trying to get it all out. "I met this quirky fellow in an alternate reality who called himself the Professor. He wants me to quit smoking, and to be a more positive role model for Karen. I know you think I'm nuts, but I need your help."

James Malone rolled out from under the truck he was working on. He gave Beth an odd smile. "You better sit down," he said. Karen sat in the folding chair next to the break table. Malone took the chair next to her and put his hand on her hand.

"This would be a Professor Emit N. Relevart," stated Malone. Beth reeled and almost lost consciousness. This day was off the charts for weirdness.

"I would strongly recommend that you follow his advice," Malone continued while patting Beth's hand. Malone's wife Susan entered the shop. She was carrying a plastic tray containing three steaming beverages. She gave them both a big smile.

"French vanilla coffee with one cream," Susan said, and handed her husband a mug. "Your favorite drink, well, that is according to our mutual friend; the Professor." Jimbo Malone gave his wife a big smile as he accepted the mug.

"Beth," Susan said, as she handed Beth a mug. "Orange cinnamon tea with one sugar, for energy." Susan laughed; Beth giggled.

"How did you know?" Beth asked. She took the mug and took a sip. "It tastes divine."

"Well let's just say that our mutual friend recommended it," said Susan Malone. "And now, my favorite," she said, taking the remaining mug. She took the tray and threw it to the side. It instantly disappeared. Karen sat next to her mom in a folding chair at the break table. She looked around in fascinated wonder. Today turned out to be a really great day.

***

The Professor looked out from his perch in an alternate reality. He took out his little black book and turned to the page that had Beth and Karen's name on it. He wrote made it a couple of extra decades by Beth's name. In parenthesis he wrote turned out to be a great mom and a excellent grandma. By Karen's name the Professor just wrote Matriarch. He smiled as he envisioned all the future generations. Putting his book away he rubbed his face. His next assignment made him very nervous. He was going to visit his mortal self in the year 2001.

## *Character*

Hilary was already having a bad day when she exited the freeway and headed toward home.

"Damn all writers," she muttered under her breath and then looked apologetically skyward.

It had been a very rough time at the job interview. Now that she and Jack, her husband, had decided that she should go back to work, all the job opportunities had disappeared.

"What else could go wrong," Hilary muttered while turning down her home street. Her answer was quick in coming.

"Oh my God!" she screamed when she saw the flames engulfing her house. "I must save Joey!"

She floored the station wagon, bumped up over the curve, and came to a screeching halt on her front lawn. For a frantic second she fought with the seatbelt, then flung the door open, and sprinted for her front porch. As she ran for the front door she collided with the soot encrusted, tear streaked, baby sitter.

"Where is Joey?" Hilary screamed.

"Upstairs in the playroom, I couldn't get him out," wailed the teenage babysitter.

Hilary stepped to the side of the porch and looked up at the playroom window. There was Joey, face plastered against the window, terrified, and screaming. She could see flames licking the air behind him.

"Move," Hilary said as she pushed the babysitter aside and rushed through the front door. The heat was intense. As she fought toward the stairway, there was an explosion from the kitchen. A giant fireball traveled down the hall and knocked her against the front wall. Her hair was singed, and her sweater had caught fire. It was so hard to breath, and the heat, it was like Hell itself. Hillary crawled through the open front door.

Shock, fear, and pain welled through her body. She had to save Joey. If only Jack were here, but Jack was at work. She would have to do this alone. A wave of panic struck her as she thought of going back into that inferno. Joey was her only child, the miracle baby, they called him. He had to be saved. Another wave of panic shot through her body.

They had tried to have children for eight years. Just when they had given up trying, bang, she was pregnant. Hilary thought back on the fourteen torturous hours of labor. She remembered the utter joy when they laid little Joey in her arms. The labor had been worth it. The wait had been worth it. Now little Joey was in trouble, and had to be saved. Pain racked through her body again.

This was not the first time Joey had been in trouble. Although he was only four, he had been at death's door on several occasions. Hilary thought back on the last time. Joey had wandered into the swimming pool and almost drowned. She had saved him then, and she would save him now. More pain racked her body, especially where the sweater had melted into her left side. The fireball had hit her there. Then the idea struck her, the pool. She could wrap herself in the beach blanket, jump in the pool, completely saturate, and then brave through the fire to save Joey. Fighting back the bile in her throat, she struggled to her feet.

The babysitter and Jack were staring at her. Firemen were lounging around in the street, smoking cigarettes. She turned toward the house. It was a pile of burnt rubble, with Joey's charred skeleton heaped on the top, a beacon of her failure.

"What the hell is wrong with you?" Asked the babysitter. "You have been spaced out for the last several hours."

"Not my fault," said Hilary.

"What, were you stuck in a sequel?" Asked the babysitter.

"Look," exclaimed Hilary. "I'm just a fictional character; it is that stupid writer's fault."

"Icks nay on the iter wray, sweetheart," cautioned Jack.

"No, you icks nay," said Hilary with real irritation. "He does a classical, by the book, scene-sequel-scene, when the situation clearly called for a scene to scene action. Hell, even a transition would have worked better than this. The man is a complete imbecile."

"Honey, please," said Jack. "Let's not offend the good author."

Hilary picked up a hammer and started hitting herself in the head.

"Oh, real mature," she said looking up, while continuing to hit herself in the head with a hammer.

"I warned you," said Jack.

"Hey, you all are lucky," chimed in the buxom babysitter. "At least you all are specific characters for this one story. I'm the generic babysitter. I'm in a lot of his work. It's no picnic, believe you, me."

"Ladies, please," cautioned Jack.

"Well, I'm tired of it," complained the babysitter. "Not only is he a jackass, but he's a pervert too. You wouldn't believe some of the things he has me do. In fact, last Saturday night, after his wife had gone to bed, he had me...."

The hammer turned into a chainsaw, and Hilary made quick work of the babysitter, silencing her forever, or at least until she was needed again.

"Hilary," Jack whined. "Let's just cut our losses, and be thankful."

"Thankful!" Hilary wheeled on Jack, the chainsaw revving.

"Yes," Jack said, his voice calm. "Thankful for such a great and talented writer."

The chainsaw disappeared.

"Thankful, that this is a 1040-word writing competition, and not a 90,000 word novel." Jack was whispering now.

Hilary giggled.

"Thankful that it's Saturday night, the author has had several beers, and he will be asleep soon." He was barely whispering now.

Hilary nodded in understanding. In a low whisper, she asked, "Should we transition, now?"

Jack nodded.

Three hours later.

"Did you make it?" Hilary asked.

"I'm here," Jack whispered, putting his finger up to his mouth. "He's sleeping like a baby."

Hilary smiled. "We should send this off, before he..." Hilary pointed up to the sky. "...wakes up and has a chance to edit it."

"It would serve the bastard right," said Jack.

They both giggled, and looked deep into each other's eyes.

"I love you, Jack," whispered Hilary.

"I love you, too," whispered Jack.

They held hands, and silently, oh so very silently, left the scene.

The End.

## *Whoops!*

I don't remember much about my death. The roads were icy and I was speeding. I was half-way through the skid before I even realized anything was wrong. Instinctively I hit my brakes. That just seemed to make things worse. Then I was through the guard rail and falling. Next came a period of darkness.

Here is where the story gets interesting. I awoke outside the Pearly Gates. As a Christian I had seen many an artist rendition of them and most of them were pretty close. There was a cloud covered floor, twenty-foot-high golden fence with arched pearl inlaid gates, and angels complete with harps flying overhead. Saint Peter was standing out front, and ushered me over to a large group of people. I have no concept of how time flows in Heaven. I don't know if this group represented days or decades. But it was an interesting group for it contained; the Pope, the head of the Mormon Church, three television evangelist, twelve Baptist Ministers, a church deacon who was also the town butcher, four Jehovah Witnesses, a rabbi, and myself. All twenty-four of us just stood around talking for what seemed like a short time. Then Saint Peter called for our attention as this hippie looking fellow in a robe walked through the gates. A hush fell over our group as the hippie held up his arms for silence and we could see the nail holes in his hands.

"My friends," Jesus began. "My father will meet you soon and pass his judgment. But first you must take one more test. Good luck."

Jesus gestured to a point behind us. We all turned to look. As the clouds cleared we could see a picnic ground complete with barbeque pit. On the picnic table were coolers full of wine. A cow stood grazing next to the barbeque pit. When we turned back, Jesus and Saint Peter were both gone.

The deacon who was also a butcher was the first one to the picnic grounds. He made fast work of the cow. A couple of the Jehovah Witnesses got the fire going. The Pope and the Rabi both blessed the wine. We all pitched in on the cooking. Before long we had us a pretty good barbeque going. Not all of us drank the wine, but we all sure enjoyed the steaks. There is no hunger in Heaven. There is also no fullness. The steaks tasted good. Heavenly, if you pardon the pun. So we all had several.

The Pope was the first to see him and immediately asserted his leadership.

"Stop," the Pope commanded. "That boy, he is our test."

He pointed to a small emaciated lad of about ten standing on the outskirts of the picnic area. The boy wore a torn loin cloth. It appeared he had neither eaten nor bathed in a very long time. We all rushed to him and brought him to the picnic table. Then we tried to outdo each other with hospitality toward the boy. We fed him steaks and even gave him some wine. Congratulating ourselves, we went back to eating. We didn't see Jesus enter. He kind of startled us.

"Come," Jesus said. "The test is over. It is time to meet the creator, the one and true God."

Smiling and very proud of ourselves we filed through the Pearly Gates, right behind Jesus. The more important people jostled for up front. Somehow, the boy and I ended up in the back. I shrugged, grabbed the boy's hand and took my place at the end of the line. We started up the great columned steps that lead into a giant golden castle.

As we entered the great hall I could hear screaming. The boy and I were bowled over by the Pope who was running in the opposite direction. Struggling to our feet, we were knocked down again by the head of the Mormon Church, who was also screaming. His hair had turned white. The Jehovah Witnesses and Baptist Ministers came rushing out next. They were screaming and tearing at their hair and clothes. The boy and I finally entered the castle where we saw the television ministers sitting on the floor banging their heads against the wall. They were babbling incoherently. The Deacon was laughing hysterically and gouging his own eyes out.

I held tightly to the boy's hand and we entered the great hall. Angels playing harps lined the walls. A bright light radiated from up ahead. We approached the throne and then we understood. There sat God. She was a cow.

The End

## *Flower Effect*

"Can we go walking in the graveyard, Grandpa?" Alyssa asked. She was tugging on his arm. "Please," she begged. She was still clutching the flower her Sunday school teacher had given her at church that morning.

"Okay, okay," said Grandpa. He was never any good at telling her no. "You are, without a doubt, the strangest child I know."

"Thank you, Grandpa," Alyssa said, giving him a sly smile.

Grandpa wasn't sure if she where thanking him for agreeing to go to the graveyard, or for calling her strange. It was probably both, but with Alyssa you never knew. She definitely lived in her own little world. He tussled her long curly hair.

"Can we take the motorcycle?" She asked.

"Absolutely not," said Grandpa. "We are less than three hundred yards away, and you are still in your good Sunday dress."

"Alright," Alyssa said. Apparently she was giving in on this issue without a fight. Her face was etched in deep concentration as she leaped into the air turning circles. She held the flower at arm's length, and stared at it while she jumped her air circles. After ten turns she stopped, and looked up at Grandpa.

"Can we go now? She asked. She had a look of controlled annoyance on her face.

"Let me grab my hat," said Grandpa with a sigh. "I was waiting on you."

Walking hand in hand, they exited the back gate of Grandpa's apartment complex, crossed the street, and entered the forty-acre cemetery. As normal on a Sunday afternoon, the graves were covered in fresh flowers. The town's unwritten ritual was to visit departed loved ones directly after church. Flowers were a must. In a town of eight thousand, they boasted five flower shops. Flowers were everywhere.

"Oh, how pretty," said Alyssa pointing to a grave decked out with three floral arrangements. She read the name on the headstone. "James Morris must be really loved."

"I guess so," said Grandpa, squeezing her hand. They turned a corner, and headed up another row.

"How sad," whimpered Alyssa. Her face wrinkled up with emotion, and she began to silently cry. "He has no flowers. No one loves him today." Tears were starting to stream down her face.

Grandpa felt a twinge of emotion also. Not over the stupid flowers. Grandpa was probably the only person in town who did not get thrilled over flowers. No, Grandpa was chocked up over his Granddaughter. She was truly the strangest little girl he had ever met, but she was also the most loving, caring, kindest person he had ever known.

"Yes, that is sad precious," he said, putting his hand on her shoulder.

Alyssa looked down at the grave, and then at the flower in her hand.

"I'm going to give him my flower," she said. She laid the flower down at the base of the headstone. "There you go Ted Jones, husband, born 8 November 1956, and died 18 December 2001. Now you are loved today also." Her forehead wrinkled. "Hmmm, that made you only forty-five when you died."

Grandpa thought for a while. About twice as long as his Granddaughter did. "That's right. Incredible. You are very smart for a six-year-old."

Alyssa smiled, and took his hand as they started walking again. She gave one glance back.

After a moment, Grandpa said, "That was a very good deed. I know how much that flower meant to you."

Alyssa was beaming now. Grandpa was always surprised at how fast a child's emotions could change. She was skipping next to him now.

"My Sunday school teacher said that no good deed goes unrewarded, because the deed itself is its own reward."

Grandpa chuckled to himself as he reflected back on his sixty-two years of life. Twenty-two of those years he had spent in the Army, and that included fighting in three wars. Inwardly he thought. That is the difference between us, and I hope you can always stay pure. But I had learned that saying as, no good deed goes unpunished.

Out loud, Grandpa said, "That is a very good saying, precious."

\*\*\*

Bernice pulled into the cemetery at nine o'clock Monday morning. "Thank God, no one is here," she muttered under her breath. That was why she had picked Monday morning as the time, on those rare occasions, when she did visit her husband's grave. She hated people, and Monday morning was the best chance of not having to see anybody in the cemetery.

She had moved here from New York City, right after her husband's death. Not that she had any love for this town, but it was over a thousand miles away, and it had a hick police force. She had, after all, murdered her husband. He had deserved it. He had broken his marriage vows, and cheated on her. So, she had poisoned him, and had his body interned in his home town. Well, it wasn't really his home town, but no one in New York City could possible know that.

He had strayed, just like her first husband had. So, like her first husband, Ted had to die. He had been a lot cleverer though. She had never actually caught Ted cheating, but she knew. She saw the way those women would glance at him. All casual like, so they wouldn't raise her suspicions. They thought they were being so clever. There were also those times when he was late coming home from work. When she confronted him, he acted like he didn't know what she was talking about. That was a trick her first husband had used, even when she had caught him red handed.

Yes, Ted was clever, but not clever enough. He had eaten a poison laced Valentines meal. Didn't see that one coming, did you Teddy boy? Then she had taken care of those six sluts who lived in the same apartment complex as them. Each one in a different way, so that the police wouldn't become too suspicious. Still, it was safer to move on.

One thing bothered her though. Her new neighbor, Sara. Sara had brought her a cake when she first moved down here. She even shed a tear or two when she had told Sara her husband was dead. Why would she cry for Ted? She was also always trying to get her to talk about him. She had thrown the cake away. It was most probably poisoned.

However, Sara was only eighteen. That would have made her fourteen when Ted died. Kind of young to be traveling up to New York for a little adultery. No, Bernice thought. Sara was just a meddling busy body. An annoying girl that needed to be avoided, but not an adulteress that needed to be killed.

"I was just acting crazy," said Bernice as she pulled the car down the lane that housed Ted's grave. "That cake probably wasn't poisoned."

"You whore," Bernice shouted as she slammed the car door shut. "You almost got away with it! You almost fooled me!" Then in a quieter voice she muttered, "You didn't know I'd be going to the grave today. That's where you made your mistake girly. You left him a flower. Only a lover would do that, and that means you must die."

## *Homecoming*

The Nevels were very proud. It had been a long eight months for Tom and Linda, but Joe was finally coming home. He was also coming home a hero, according to the letter they had received from the Department of the Army. Joe had earned several medals while fighting in Iraq. In their community of a little over a thousand people, only three had actually signed up for military service since the horrors of September eleventh.

Everybody had talked about it. I mean hell, it was the number one topic of conversation, but only three had signed up. Of those three only Joe had volunteered for Infantry duty in the United States Army. The Nevels had a lot to be proud of, and now Joe was coming home.

They had gotten the letter in today's mail. Joe was supposed to call when he got to San Francisco on the eighth, and that was tomorrow. He should be home two days after that. That gave them just three days to plan, organize, and put together Joe's homecoming celebration. It would be a grand affair with a parade and a big banquet. The whole town would be involved. Linda immediately started making phone calls. Tom went to see the Mayor to arrange the use of the town hall.

Linda had just finished reading Betty, her neighbor, the typed letter she had received from Joe, when the call waiting tone beeped in. Checking the caller ID she noticed an unfamiliar area code.

Thinking it could be from Joe, she signed off with Betty and took the call.

"Hello," Linda said. She was suddenly nervous.

"Mom," Joe's voice resounded through the receiver. Tears came to Linda's eyes.

"Joe," she said. "It is so great to hear from you. We love you so much. We have missed you so much. We are so proud of you. You must have gotten home early. When are you coming home?"

"Tomorrow," Joe said. His voice had a sad and tired tone to it.

"Oh Joe," Linda beamed. "That will be great. We have to work fast here now. Nancy, your old girlfriend will be glad to see you. She has been seeing that good for nothing Alex, but when my war hero son comes home, and the whole town turns out for the celebration, well, she'll come running back to you. We are having this big celebration, with parades and speeches. We will have to move it up because you're coming home early and…"

"Mom," Joe interrupted. "I don't want a celebration. I need to ask you something."

"No celebration," Linda quipped. "That's nonsense. There will be a parade, and you

marching as the guest of honor. There will be…."

"Mom," Joe interrupted again. "I must ask you something."

"Okay son," said Linda. "Ask your question, and then we can get back to planning your celebration, and knock off all this other silliness."

Joe took a deep breath, let out a sigh, and began, "I have a buddy, an Army friend who I want to bring home with me. He has nowhere else to go."

"Well sure son," Linda said. "We can put him up at the hotel."

"Mom," Joe jumped in. "He can't stay at the hotel. He was pretty badly injured in the war. He needs someone to take care of him."

At that moment Tom came home. Linda motioned him over to her.

"Hold on Joe," she said. "Your Dad is here." To Tom she whispered, "Pick up the other phone, it's Joe. He wants to bring home a wounded war buddy."

Tom picked up the other line and said, "Joe, it's so great to talk to you. We are so very proud of you. We have got big plans for when you get home. Now what is this your Mom is saying about a wounded war buddy?"

Joe began again, "Mom, Dad. He has nowhere else to go. His Bradley was hit by a missile. He lost both his legs, he is horrible burned on his face and upper body, and he is blind."

There was a long moment of silence. Linda was staring at Tom with a look of deep concern. Finally Tom said, "Joe, this is quite the burden. This fellow would need constant care. How long do you plan on keeping him?"

There was another silence, shorter this time, and then Joe said, "Well Dad, he has nowhere else to go. He would stay with us indefinitely." Linda let out a gasp.

"Joe," Tom said. "I understand you wanting to take care of your war buddy. It is very commendable, but you do realize what a horrible burden this would be?" Doesn't the Army have facilities to take care of people like this? I mean, I feel for his loss, and yours too son, but you've got a life. This shouldn't have to be our problem."

Linda chimed in with, "We don't mean to be cruel, but that would totally rearrange all our lives. Especially, yours, son."

There was another short silence, and then Joe said, "I understand, but I had to ask."

Tom jumped in, "Please don't be mad at us son."

"No," Joe said. "In fact I'm actually a little relieved. That is a big weight off my shoulders. I'll see you tomorrow, I love you."

"We love you too, and are so proud of you," Linda and Tom said together.

When the line went dead, Linda looked at Tom with deep concern etched on her face.

"It's okay," said Tom. "War changes people, but he will be okay. It is best this way." Tom and Linda hugged. It was a deep desperate hug. It was the first time they hugged like that since September eleventh.

The strangeness of the phone call was forgotten as Tom and Linda leaped into their chores of preparing for the homecoming celebration. It was past midnight when they fell exhausted into bed, but they somehow managed to muster the energy to make love.

That was something else they hadn't done in a long time, since before September eleventh.

Tom and Linda were awakened at nine o'clock the next morning by the doorbell. Every thirty seconds thereafter came a firm three raps knocked. The knock had an authoritarian and infinitely patient air to it. It was very spooky. Within a couple of minutes Tom and Linda had roused themselves, grabbed robes and rushed downstairs.

What greeted them was not their son, but an Army officer decked out in full dress uniform. They let him in, and he ushered them to take a seat in their own living room. They complied without hesitation. The Army Officer remained standing.

Ma'am, Sir," the officer began. "My name is Captain Tousinski, United States Army. On Behalf of the President of the United States, and the Secretary of The Army, "it is with the deepest condolence that we inform you of the death of your son, Specialist-four Joseph P. Nevel."

At this point Linda gasped and clutched her chest. Tom stiffened and his eyes became moist. The Captain continued without interruption, "Recipient of the Silver Star, the Purple Heart, Army Commendation Medal, and the Combat Infantryman's Badge. His loss will be greatly felt by this nation."

There was a long pause. Finally Tom meekly asked, "But how? We just talked to him yesterday."

The Captain softened his stance and expression a bit. He almost looked human for a moment. "It was yesterday afternoon, sir, it was a suicide. His body will be flown in tonight. I am the notification officer, a causality assistance officer……"

Captain Tousinski paused and pulled out a business card, and handed it to Tom. Then he continued, "A Captain Tim Ryan will arrive with the body. He will assist you in any way possible. He will have the answers to your questions."

Sometime during the long silence, Captain Tousinski turned and walked away. Tom and Linda did not register hearing the door close. They sat in shocked silence.

They were not any better composed as they waited for the C130 airplane, carrying Joe's body, to taxi to a halt, and open its back ramp. Linda rocked back and forth clutching an imaginary infant Joe while muttering, "My baby," over and over again.

Tom spent all his effort fighting back tears. A young officer in Dress Greens departed the plane and approached them.

"Ma'am, Sir," he said while glancing at each of them in turn.

"My name is Captain Ryan, on behalf of the…"

"Enough Captain," Tom cut him off. "We'd like to see the body. We just talked to our son yesterday. He seemed fine then. Maybe the Army has made some kind of horrible mistake."

Captain Ryan considered for a moment, shrugged, and said, "Yes sir, please follow me sir."

They approached a coffin draped in an American flag. Captain Ryan removed the flag, opened the coffin, and stepped aside.

Although the face was badly burned, they could easily recognize their son, Joe. Tom was the first to understand the gravity of what had happened. Being a war veteran himself he accepted it, and dealt with it with a steady stream of silent tears originating from his aching soul. Linda was a little slower on the uptake. When realization finally dawned on her she handled it with hysterical wailing, and threw herself on the coffin that contains their son Joe. Joe's corpse was legless, horrible burned on his face and upper body, and missing both his eyes.

## *Rally*

QB4017 looked at herself in the mirror as she put on her state issue undergarments. They were type II, the binding kind. She stopped, removed the top piece and looked at herself in profile. A voluptuous body reflected back from the mirror. She smiled. She had her Grandma's figure. What was it they used to call her, their African American Princess? It had been a long time since she had been known by anything other than QB4017. As she stared at herself in the mirror, her thoughts drifted back in time to when she had last seen her grandparents. It was at a picnic, thirty years ago. The day before the "Great Liberation and Equality for All."

"Hello my African American Princess. Ready for a hamburger?" Grandpa asked.

"Sure, Grandpa, with lots of ketchup," she responded.

Grandpa scooped up a burger off the grill and plopped it on a toasted bun. He then added a very liberal amount of ketchup and handed it to her.

"Thanks Grandpa," she said.

"No problem, sodas are in the cooler." Grandpa grabbed a hamburger for himself and headed to the cooler to get a beer.

As they fished out their drinks, Grandpa said, "Princess, we have some serious talking to do. Times are changing, and we want to share some things with you. Let's go sit next to Grandma."

They sat at the picnic table and Grandma handed her a plate with potato chips on it. Grandma looked at Grandpa and then they both looked at her.

"Princess," Grandpa started. "God has made each of us special. Everyone in the whole world is special in their own special way. Never be ashamed of what you are. You have strengths and you have weaknesses. Both are beautiful. Both are what make you special. Now, remember that you are an American of African descent."

"And a woman," chimed in Grandma.

"Yes," continued Grandpa. "A woman and black. That has its strengths, and that has its limitations. But that is you, and that is special."

"Very special," said Grandma.

"Now Princess," Grandpa said "A new political group has taken over. They want us all to be equal. Their intentions are good, but they have this policy known as zero tolerance."

QB4017 was jolted back to the present by the blaring of the warning horn.

"Inequality," she cursed. She only had ten minutes to make the Trans.

She quickly clamped on the top part of her undergarments and slipped on her gray jumper. She rubbed her hand over her shaved head to check that it met state hygiene standards and headed for the door.

She boarded the Trans on time and joined the sea of shaved heads and gray jumpers. They were all QBs on this Trans. Most of them were going to work in section four. She strapped in to her assigned slot.

QB4017 felt a little depressed. She always did after thinking about her grandparents, especially that last picnic. She missed them. It was also the last time she had eaten a hamburger, or drank a soda. Probably for the best. The state said those things were bad for you. That was why now you only ate healthy foods.

QB4017 roused herself from her depression. Tonight was the rally. This would be her first time being eligible to go. Maybe QB4999 would be there.

"Are you going to the rally," she asked the gray jumper next to her?

"Ah no, not eligible," came the nervous masculine reply.

"Thank you citizen," she said, regaining her composure.

That was okay. Tonight she would be able to talk to people freely at the rally. The rally was the place where you could find a mate. If her calculations were correct, than QB4999 would be there. Now that would be a great mate. She giggled, and then caught herself. Her spirits were soaring as the Trans came to a stop in front of her office building.

In the hallway she ran into QB4999.

"Good morning QB4999," she said.

"Good morning QB4017," QB4999 replied, a broad smile on his face.

"Are you going to the rally tonight?" she asked.

"Yes I am," QB4999 replied. His smile widened.

"So am I," she said. Her heart raced and she felt giddy. "I look forward to seeing you there. You look very nice today."

QB4999's white skin had turned very pale. He turned to the camera on the wall and stated, "I took no offense by that; I look forward to seeing you there." Then he hurried off.

QB4017 was dazed. What had she done? This wasn't fair. She started to cry as she walked to her office.

\*\*\*

QB4999 was also crying. He was already in his office with the door closed. He had had a crush on QB4017 since he had first met her three years ago. Now she had made a terrible blunder. She could be terminated.

"QB4999," the speaker on his desk blared.

"Yes control," he solemnly replied.

"The state has filed a sexual harassment grievance in your behalf. Zero tolerance. Justice will be done," the speaker barked.

QB4999's head reeled. This couldn't be happening. It was too horrible. But maybe he could do something.

"Control," he said, a little too loudly.

"Yes QB4999." There had been a few seconds delay.

"I would like to file a petition to withdraw the grievance," he stated, lowering his voice and gaining strength and confidence as he spoke. "QB4017 and I know each other very well. We were going to the rally tonight. We will probably be mates. I know the state allows certain liberties between spouses. I want this taken into consideration."

After several seconds the speaker responded with, "We will get back to you."

\*\*\*

For QB4999 and QB4017 that was the longest day of their lives. They managed to talk briefly to each other at lunch. They agreed to marry to help out the situation. They would discuss the details at the rally.

About one hour before the works end horn, QB4999 was startled by his office speaker.

"QB4999," it blared.

"Yes control," he replied.

"We have reviewed your request," the speaker said, the tone softer. "It is not uncommon for a victim to feel guilt over the crime. We have scheduled you for victim classes to help you overcome this problem. We request that you withdraw your petition."

QB4999 leaped to his feet and screamed, "No! You can't do this. I won't withdraw my petition."

More seconds passed and the speaker replied, "Very well. Your petition to withdraw your grievance will be reviewed in seven days. You will attend victim classes starting now. Your eligibility for the rally has been revoked."

QB4999 sat down with relief. This could work. At least he had bought some time. He was sure he could hold out for seven days of victim class indoctrination. Besides, there were other ways to get married besides the rally.

\*\*\*

"Yes control," he finally said.

Ten minutes later, QB4017 was startled as two blue jumpers entered her office. She shakily got to her feet. Without a word they grabbed her, one to each arm, and escorted her out of the building. They walked the one block to the control headquarters building and entered through the back entrance. She started to struggle when they entered a room containing a vaporizer.

"No," she screamed! "You don't understand. It's okay. Look, Grandpa said we were all special. It's okay to be special. I'm special, QB4999 is special. We are all special. It's not wrong." She was struggling harder now.

"QB4017," Blue jumper one said. "You have been found guilty of sexual harassment. Under the conditions of zero tolerance, you are to be terminated. Equality for all."

She began whimpering now. "No, I'm special. It's not wrong."

The two blue jumpers chunked her into the vaporizer. There was a loud zap, a blue flash, and the smell of ozone. Then she was gone. Her death, according to the records, was fast, painless, and most humane.

***

QB4999 was attending his last victim class when the monitor interrupted with a news bulletin.

"Justice was served last week when a defiant sexual harasser was terminated," the monitor stated. In the background of the broadcast played a continuous sound loop of QB4017 saying, 'I'm special.'

"QB4017 had been maliciously sexually harassing the workers of section four. This reign of terror is over."

"Equality for all," the broadcast ended.

A loud cheer erupted in the classroom. The instructor walked over to QB4999.

"Are you okay QB4999," the instructor asked? "Remember, it is no crime to be a victim."

QB4999 listened to the cheering in the classroom and felt their sympathy for him. Thanks to the classes, he now understood that he was the victim and that there was no shame in that.

"Yes, Citizen," he said. "I'll be alright. The National Song began to play over the speakers. QB 4999's chest began to swell. He was starting to feel vindicated. After all, he had been the victim

The End.

## *Felicia Nightingale*

"Where have you been, Corporal?" I barked at the six-foot six, three hundred pound, dark skinned, mountain of muscle that walked out of the jungle.

"Hi, L.T.," said Corporal Nightingale nonchalantly. He shook his head as if to clear it. Then his eyes came into sharp focus. "I've been having a Sunday brunch with my wife, sir."

This caused nervous giggles among the new guys and worn out smiles among the old timers. We had done this dance before.

"Would that be your dead wife?" I asked.

"Yes sir," said Nightingale. "Going on two years now, but heaven must agree with her. She is looking better every time I see her."

Some of the new guys started to laugh, not knowing how to take this. I just smiled. Corporal Nightingale was the acting Squad Leader of the second squad. With eleven months in country, he was the most senior of the platoon for time in Nam, even beating my nine-month time. He was also the best Squad Leader I had.

"You wouldn't be trying for a section eight?" I asked.

"No sir," Nightingale said thoughtfully. "My destiny is right here in the bush. In fact, if it were not for my destiny, I wouldn't be able to visit with my wife. So, I'm happy to stay right here."

"Your squad has point tonight," I said.

"I'll be ready sir," he said. Then as if by afterthought, he asked, "You ever eat Cajun food?"

My platoon was down to twenty-eight men, and all of them were listening now. I decided to put on a show.

"I am Yankee white bread, through and through," I said. "Born and raised in New York, West Point Class of sixty-eight, currently fighting to stem the tide of communist aggression."

There were some "Yeehi's, and "Arruuuga's" from the men.

"The only south I've been," I continued, "is the South Bronx, and now South Vietnam."

The men erupted in cheers.

"Too bad," said Nightingale. "My wife makes an excellent crawdad boil, and her homebrew honey beer. You'd love it."

At 2100 hours that night, the choppers picked up my platoon from base camp. Corporal Nightingale, walked point, while I positioned myself near the middle. Two miles into the patrol, Nightingale halted the patrol. I hurried up to his position.

"Looks bad, Lieutenant," he whispers, from a crouched position. "Ambush country."

I nod. "We'll bypass to the south," I say.

I had only taken two steps when, "click, whir."

I felt, more than saw, the spinning little mine known as a bouncing betty. Instantly muzzle flashes appear on the far hill side. A blinding flare goes off, and I shut my eyes to protect them from the bright light.

When I open my eyes, I am sitting at a big wooden table. I appear to be on a houseboat, moored out in a swamp. A breeze blows through the open windows. The odor is different, but not unpleasant. Nightingale is sitting across from me.

"Corporal," I say, nodding.

"Lieutenant," he nods back.

A very beautiful, mulatto women is standing next to the table. Her purple housedress accents her voluptuous body and highlights her piercing dark eyes. She has long curly raven hair that goes down to the middle of her back. With her hands on her hips, she is surveying us both.

"You can just leave that war talk outside of my house," she states. "In here we are on a first name basis. She briefly glares at her husband, who sheepishly grins. "My name is Felicia, and that is my husband, Tony. Welcome to my humble home." She extends her hand.

"I am Jim, the honor is all mine," I said, taking her hand, and kissing it. I am happy and content in this surrealistic world. I don't want to think about the fact that it is probably not real.

More members of the platoon show up, and we make our informal introductions. Felicia is a gracious host and keeps our mason jars filled with her homebrew honey beer. After Tony says the blessing, Felicia brings in a ten-gallon colander and dumps it on the table. Out come steaming new potatoes, corn on the cob, and what look like baby lobsters. I am informed they are crawfish. The corn and potatoes are delicious, and I finally got the nerve up to eat a crawfish. I pick one up and bite into its tail, crunching up the shell. Everybody is laughing.

"I see we need to teach our guest the proper way to eat crawdads," said Felicia.

She takes a fresh one, and shows me how to shuck it, and suck out the tail meat. Within an hour I am laughing, and even sucking the brains out of their heads. This is a perfect meal, and the most fun I've had in years.

When I can't eat anymore, I grab another homebrew and join Tony out on the deck.

"You have a wonderful wife," I say, sitting down beside him. "Anytime you want to do this again, its okay with me."

He looked at me with teary eyes and placed a hand on my shoulder. Then he leaned back against the house and closed his eyes. I leaned back also, looked out over the swamp, and closed my eyes.

The next time I opened my eyes, I could see helicopter blades whirling above me. I was lying on a medical litter. From my peripheral vision I could see we were flying at tree top level. I could hear explosions, and anti-aircraft guns all around me. My whole body hurt. My legs felt like they were on fire. I closed my eyes tight. I wanted to be anywhere but here. I wanted to go back to Felicia's, and Tony's houseboat.

The doctors say it was a delusion brought on by post traumatic stress syndrome. The severity of my injuries, the loss of my legs, the death of every member of my platoon while under my command, has traumatized me to the point that I have created a dream world. When I identified a picture of Felicia, a woman I had never seen before, the doctors looked at me with skepticism. Finally, they agreed that I had transplanted those memories, after seeing the picture. They said that the woman in my dream houseboat has now changed, in my mind to the one in the picture. I almost believed them. However, I am keeping one piece of evidence away from the doctors. I couldn't stand to have them explain that away. Sometimes the pain in my nonexistent legs is unbearable. I also burst into tears over just about anything. I haven't been able to watch a news report since returning to the states, they're just too traumatic. At times like that I grab my proof. I keep it in a glass vial, on a chain around my neck. It gives me faith in a good world, and hope for the future. It contains something I picked out of my teeth on the chopper ride to the hospital. I had it confirmed by a marine biologist. It is a piece of shell from a crawfish.

The End

www.ingramcontent.com/pod-product-compliance
Lightning Source LLC
LaVergne TN
LVHW091542070526
838199LV00002B/176